ADVENTUROUS ALI

THE ALL-SEEING EYE

TYLER H. JOLLEY
MARY H. GEIS

JOLLEY
CHRONICLES

For my daughter Olivia. If it wasn't for you these stories would have never been created. Enjoy every word while you read them. Be adventurous.

CHAPTER 1

Alison Liv Isner rushed into the storage room at Field and Excavation Inc., which also happened to be where she lived. Just two and a half weeks ago a globe in the storage area outside her room had transported her to the island of Honduras, where she had embarked on her first adventure. She'd found and returned a monkey idol to a high priest called Chuwen with the help of her new friends Figgy, Chicaletta, Bait, Glenda, and last but certainly not least, the fat rat named Tristan. It was a quest her mom had planned to undertake two years before Ali's birth, but she never had the chance due to her untimely passing.

Alison had returned to her room daily, before her archery lessons, trying to recreate that fateful day in September, but another expedition eluded her. The calendar had turned a page to the cool and colorful month of October. She pulled off her tweed jacket and tossed it behind a partially closed door in the back room. Plopping down onto the antique rug, and smoothing her two long braids behind her shoulders, she opened her mom's journal.

The next adventure was to take place in Egypt's pyramid catacombs, leading to the tomb of Pharaoh Zicobus. It was one of many quests her mom had researched and planned out but never had the chance to accomplish. She traced the strange script and sketches of the pyramids.

Pharaoh Zicobus had been a respected pharaoh who was mostly fair to his people. While it was common for pharaohs to adorn their heads with a crown, Pharaoh Zicobus's was special. His unusual headdress, according to the journal, could see the future. He'd been murdered for the special crown, but his loyal followers were able to hide it before it could be used for evil. They buried him inside a sealed secret tomb, along with his headdress.

Ali slammed the book shut and exhaled loudly. Her stomach dropped. She had to get back to her animal friends and find it before the Geese did. She still wasn't exactly sure who the Geese were, only that they weren't actual geese. They were bad people. *Very* bad people.

As Ali combed through the pages, she found a crude drawing of the headdress that her mother had sketched. It was a Nemes headdress and looked like the ones she'd seen King Tut wear in her history books. Only instead of gold and blue, it was gold and turquoise. The heavy stripes crested at the top and cascaded down past the shoulders. It was wide. Ali guessed it would be nearly even with the pharaoh's shoulders. At the top was a pyramid with an eye etched into it.

Ali knew she'd seen that symbol before. She jumped to her feet, dropped the journal on the desk, and ran to the cash register at the front of the store.

"Dad," she called. She could see the top of his head along with a customer's hat behind a row of tents.

"What are you up to, squirt?" Tommy, the only employee of Field and Excavation Inc., asked.

"Nothing." Ali avoided eye contact.

"What are you doing behind the register?"

"I need a dollar," she said.

"A dollar?" Tommy nearly yelled. "Did you ask your dad? That's a lot of money."

"I don't want to keep it," Ali said. "I just need to look at it, for a minute."

Tommy slowly made his way to the register. For sixteen he was tall, but he hadn't filled out. His lanky arms hung like two vines as he walked. He paused for just a moment and studied Ali's face before pressing a circular black button on the register. A loud ding rang out, and the cash drawer slid open. Tommy pinched a precious one-dollar bill from the till and held it above Ali's head.

"Give it to me." Ali jumped to grab it.

"Okay." He bit his lip. "Promise you'll give it back? I need this job."

"You do?" she asked. "I thought you just wanted to go to school in town."

"I'm trying to help my family." Tommy shifted. "The Dust Bowl . . . we haven't been able to farm for years."

"Oh."

"And your dad was nice enough to give me a place to sleep while I work and go to school. I owe him a lot. Just make sure you give it back, please."

"I won't even leave your sight." Ali snatched the worn bill from his hand. She flipped it over, and on the back was the same pyramid and the all-seeing eye.

"I knew it," she mumbled. "Thanks, Tommy." She handed him the bill. "I'll be in the storage room."

After running back, she opened the journal once more and stared at the headdress. Sure enough, it had the same all-seeing eye atop it. She slammed the book shut again, frustrated.

"I've got to get back there," she said.

"Back where?" Tommy surprised her.

"Um," Ali said. She slid the journal under a ledger on the nearby metal desk. "Nowhere."

"You've sure been acting weird lately, squirt." Tommy grinned. "I'm just glad you didn't knock over the pickaxes again."

It was true, in an effort to mimic everything she'd done on September 13, 1935, she had knocked over the row of pickaxes a few times. She had the bruises on her shins to prove it. But still nothing had triggered whatever it was that had taken her to Honduras.

"Sorry about that," Ali said, gently picking at the flaking paint on the desk.

"Tommy," Ali's dad yelled from the store-front. "I need you to ring up this gentleman."

"Gotta go." Tommy raised his eyebrows and left.

Ali snatched the book from its hiding place

and returned to the rug. Something on the desk caught her attention out of the corner of her eye. She turned. *The globe!* It was spinning on its own. Her heartbeat quickened, and her hands shook. Quickly thumbing to the Pharaoh Zicobus entry, she closed her eyes, pressed her palm on the journal's parchment pages, and stopped the globe with her finger.

Nothing.

She sighed.

The globe still spun slowly. All the continents began to light up like amber. She smelled the burning paper before she saw it. Hands shaking, Ali gently rotated the globe. Her eyebrow rose once she spotted the blackened continent.

Egypt.

It was just like Honduras. The edges burned to the center, and it smoked until it was completely charred and collapsed inside itself. A brilliant light shined out from the hole, as if someone had mounted a flashlight in the center of the globe.

Ali stared at it with wide eyes.

It's happening!

Vertigo forced her to sit on the rug. The room and rug spun. Her stomach cramped. She regretted her afternoon snack as the room whirled faster. She welcomed the darkness before she passed out with a smile on her face.

Alison Liv Isner embarked on her second adventure.

CHAPTER 2

Warm, dry air filled Ali's lungs, a distinct difference from the cool autumn breeze she'd grown accustomed to as of late. Her eyes flung open, and she found herself surrounded by her friends once more.

"Welcome back, love," Bait swam upside down in his mason jar that dangled from Figgy's neck.

"Human!" Figgy exclaimed. He flashed his odd, human-like grin. His cream coat was dirty with sand, his brown spots now blended in, and only his black spots stood out. Especially the one around his eye.

"I did it!" Ali nearly tripped on her own feet running over to them. "I'm back." She hugged the donkey's neck, careful not to disturb Bait's jar.

"Finally," Tristan said, poking a pink finger into his ear. "I'm sick of sand. Rats aren't built for the desert."

"I've been trying every day for over two weeks to get back." Ali took in her surroundings. The desert landscape was devoid of any life, save for a few scattered palm trees. Wind swirled sand at her feet.

"One must understand that the adventure must be ready for you, not the other way around," Chicaletta said. A slight breeze tousled her shiny golden locks.

Ali furrowed her brow. Chicaletta was a wise monkey, but Ali didn't always understand what she meant.

"I shall return," Chicaletta said, nimbly running across the desert floor.

"Are we in Egypt?" Ali asked.

"Yes, Ali, yes," Glenda yelled. "Can you even believe it?" The small bat batted her long eyelashes and smoothed her shiny coat with her wings. She stretched out a wing and examined her red-polished claws.

"No." Ali's stomach fluttered. "I can't believe I'm in Egypt."

"Believe it." Tristan scowled. "Look at all this sand!"

"Come, come," Bait said, waving a gray fin, exposing his red underbelly. "Figs, do you mind?"

Figgy, as always, was the piranha's legs. The mini burro climbed up a small sand ridge, and Ali followed. At the top, she scanned the setting. Aside from the scattered palm trees, the desert was barren. The palms were nothing like the lush ones she'd seen on her adventure in Honduras. They were tattered and sparse. To the south were old ruins. Ali squinted and could make out toppled rock columns and stone statues in the sand. One statue's arms had broken off and were partially buried in the sand at its feet. Others were missing heads or torsos, all having been subject to the harsh wind conditions.

"According to our notes," Bait said, "the head-dress should be somewhere in there." His tiny gray fin pointed to the toppled columns. "Does your mother's journal concur?"

Ali flipped open and scanned the page. "Yes, I *concur*."

"Chicaletta is doing some recon right now to confirm," Figgy said.

"Straight east, over by those pyramids, are the Geese," Bait said.

Ali's stomach flip-flopped.

"The Geese were here when we arrived," Bait said. "They're on the same mission, it would seem. However, if our notes are correct, they're in the wrong area."

Ali's friends had only made mention of the Geese. She squinted again, and Figgy bumped her thigh with his rump. "Human, there are bin-oculars in my pack."

Ali rummaged for a few minutes and found them. She uncapped the lenses and peered into the distance. Men with headdresses made from white goose feathers were digging furiously at the base of the pyramid. Some wore entire hollowed-out geese bodies on their heads. Around their necks were necklaces made from goose bills and feet all strung together.

Their pants were made of feathers that fluttered in the wind. The men were shirtless with tan backs glistening with sweat. All in all, they looked savage. Something about them didn't sit well with Ali.

"Why do they dress like that?" Ali asked. "And what do they want with the pharaoh's headdress?"

"Ali," Bait paused, "they seek to gain control of it, of the world really."

Figgy released a loud breath from his nose. His lips flapped.

"All you need to know," Bait said, "is that they are dangerous. Come, Figaro, let's return to camp."

Ali walked down the ridge, slipping on the

unstable ground every few feet. The wind slapped gritty sand against their faces. She licked the grit from her teeth.

"Are the Geese still at the pyramids?" Glenda asked.

"Yup," Figgy said.

"Awesome," Glenda smiled. Her red lipstick made her fangs look even whiter. She was the prettiest bat Ali had ever seen.

"Chicaletta should return soon," Bait said.

"I hope she brings back some steak," Tristan said.

"Brilliant idea," Bait chuckled. "Let's discuss this expedition while we make dinner."

Thoughts bounced around in Ali's mind. So, she sat and gathered them.

"We'll leave first thing tomorrow," Bait said. "We must work quickly and be sure to enter the temple unnoticed. If the Geese see us, they'll surely send a few of their men over to investigate or, at the very least, harass us."

Chicaletta cleared her throat, announcing

her return to camp.

"Or kill us," Tristan mumbled.

"That is the *last* thing we need," Glenda squeaked. "Can you imagine if they recovered the headdress first? If they could see the future?"

"Right," Bait continued, "we're sure to encounter some obstacles designed to keep grave robbers out."

"Is that what we are?" Ali asked. "Burglars of the dead?"

"Of course not!" Glenda gasped.

"Alison," Chicaletta's calloused hand grasped her shoulder, "we are saving the headdress. For if it were to fall into the wrong hands, the outcome would be disastrous. We will deliver it to Chuwen, the high priest, and he will know what to do."

"Chuwen?" Ali bit the inside of her lip. "The small man I gave the monkey idol to in Honduras? Does he follow us everywhere? Is he here now?"

"He is exactly where he is destined, and he

will appear when the adventure is complete." Chicaletta blinked slowly. "We will know we are at the right place when we hear the drums, just as we will know we have succeeded with the same drums."

Ali didn't answer. Her insides shook like she was cold. But that was impossible from the desert heat. She had longed for another adventure, but with the Geese involved she wasn't sure anymore. They tracked and chased them to try and steal the monkey idol in Honduras. Plus, they were the reason for the Dust Bowl. But Ali didn't know how they did that. With every artifact they stole, they exploited and wreaked havoc on the whole earth. This was no game. The world depended on her.

"Hey, before we give it to the priest," Tristan plopped down and folded his arms, "I'd like to use it to see when I'm finally going to eat."

Ali burst out laughing and patted the top of his black head. He pushed her finger away and scowled, then jumped up and scurried toward the tent. She followed him into the large rectangle tent, the smell of spicy food beckoning to them.

"Bon appétit," Glenda said. "Dinner is totally served."

"How did you make that so fast?" Ali asked, her eyes wide.

Glenda giggled in response.

Ali fixed herself a plate of rice and beans. She was so anxious she didn't remember what it tasted like, only that her stomach was full and her plate was empty. Chicaletta nodded her head toward the back area of the tent, and Ali followed her to a cot with clothes folded neatly, just like before. *Perfect size for me.* The only difference was the crossbow already waiting for her on the ground next to her boots.

"Alison," Chicaletta lifted Ali's face with a finger under her chin, "you are as strong as they come. Just like your mother. Now you must be as brave as we believe you to be. Sleep well, my child."

She shivered. Wise wisdom from a wise monkey.

Nervous, she settled on sleeping in her adventure clothes just in case. The last time she'd slept in her clothes was the day before the spelling bee. The ritual gave her comfort. The sides of the tent clapped loudly from the wind outside. She placed her shoes on top of her hat, then crawled into her sleeping bag.

Alison Liv Isner went to sleep with a lump in her throat.

CHAPTER 3

Ali awoke to an irritating patter against her face.

"Not now, Tristan." Ali rolled over.

"Me? Why do you always assume *I* did something?" Tristan jumped onto her chest.

Ali blinked a few times and saw that the culprit behind her discomfort wasn't the rat but rather gritty sand whipping across her face. The door of the canvas tent had become completely untied overnight and flapped in the strong wind. Sand swirled around them.

"It's a haboob!" Tristan yelled. Still on Ali's chest, he lay on his stomach, and propped his chin on his fist.

"Ha-what?" She squinted and wiped the sand and sleep from her face.

"Ha*boob*." Tristan rolled onto his back and laughed. "Haboob, haboob, haboob," he laughed again.

"Morning, human," Figgy interrupted. "Tristan's right, it's called a haboob. It's like a blizzard. But there's no snow; it's basically a storm made of sand and dust."

"Like the one back home," Ali whispered, thinking of the terrible Dust Bowl that plagued most of the United States.

"Haboob!" Tristan was laughing so hard he rolled off Ali and landed with a heavy thud on the floor.

"Yes, yes, Tristan," Bait said. "Now come along. Let's get moving. I estimate this is just the beginning of the storm. Look." He pointed with a fin toward the west.

A wall of sand and dust engulfed the sky and land. A cold sweat ran down Ali's spine. The dry air blasted dust on her and clung to her exposed skin. She rolled her thin white sleeves down and buttoned the cuff.

"Come on, Figgy," Glenda called. "You know the drill."

Figgy trotted toward the front of the tent as Chicaletta made her way toward the back. She held out both hands. In one was a muffin, and in the other was a set of dust goggles.

"Eat," she said to Ali. "Then wrap your mosquito veil around your face and secure your goggles over your eyes to hold it in place. Protect your eyes."

"Chicaletta, this headdress, do you have a picture?"

The golden lion tamarin tapped her temple.

"There's a drawing in my mom's journal. It has an all-seeing eye at the top. Is that what makes it magical?"

"Perhaps, or not." Chicaletta smiled. "What makes it special is not of our concern. Keeping it safe is."

Ali gobbled up the plain bran muffin in a few bites and quickly wrapped her scarf around her head and mouth. With her hat already secured she struggled to get the goggles over the brim. Finally, she had them firmly in place over her eyes. Her vision was obstructed, but that was nothing compared to the sandstorm taking place.

"Ready?" Glenda's high-pitched voice cut through the wind.

Ali turned.

Once again everything was packed and condensed onto Figgy's back. Her mouth fell agape.

"How?" she mumbled through the veil.

"I told you before." Glenda landed on Chicaletta's shoulder and firmly planted her claws into her fur. "We have a system."

Chicaletta secured her goggles over her face, then helped Figgy with his own. Glenda's goggles, of course, were horn-rimmed with jewels and looked like she'd just stepped out of Hollywood. She quickly touched up her red lipstick, but sand stuck to it.

"A little help, love," Bait said.

"Sure." Ali's voice was muffled.

"There's a leather cloth near the top of the pack." He tapped on the jar. "Would you tie it around the top of my jar? I don't want any sand getting into the air holes."

Ali nodded and searched the pack on Figgy's back. A worn leather cloth the size of a handkerchief was lying on top of the cook pot. She unscrewed the ring, lifted the metal top with holes in it, placed the leather over the jar, and finally replaced the lid and ring.

She chuckled.

Normally when she unscrewed a mason jar it was for jelly on toast.

"Thank you, love," Bait said with a stifled voice.

Chicaletta tied a rope around Ali's waist, and before she could protest Tristan scurried up her leg and squeezed himself in a loop on her utility belt.

"What?" Tristan crossed his arms and looked up at her. "I'm a perfect fit. And I'm bound to get blown away out there. I could *die*, you know."

Ali laughed and patted his head with her index finger. Tristan almost wiggled himself free trying to dodge the affection.

She clasped the rope that was around her waist. "What's this for, Chicaletta?"

"One must always be prepared." Chicaletta nodded her head toward the storm. Then she tied the rope around herself and Figgy. "We will stay together until we are out of the storm and at the pyramid's opening. Do you have your compass, Ali?"

"Yes." She rummaged in her belt and pulled it free.

"Find one hundred and thirty-one degrees southeast. That should lead us directly to the entrance. I measured the location out yesterday," Chicaletta said.

Ali fumbled with it a few seconds before dropping it into the ground. With shaking hands, she quickly bent and plucked it out of the sand before it got buried. With the tent packed, Ali realized the intensity of the storm. Bait was right. It was only getting worse.

"Got it," she said. Fine particles beat against the veil over her ears. That, coupled with the raging wind, made it hard to hear anything. "It's a good thing you found the coordinates yesterday. This storm is making it impossible to see five feet in front of you."

The wind howled and spat dust all over them.

"This storm," Chicaletta yelled, "is a lucky omen."

"Lucky?" Ali yelled back.

"The haboob is preventing the Geese from seeing us."

"And it's totally covering our footprints," Glenda squeaked.

Ali's heart dropped. She'd nearly forgotten about the Geese. Unfamiliar with haboobs and how long they lasted, she kept a hand on the rope. Looking back a few times to ensure everyone was still with her, she noticed that Glenda was no longer gripping Chicaletta's shoulder.

She gasped, sucking in her scarf.

"Where's Glenda?" she yelled, spitting out the scarf. Ali could barely hear her own voice over the raging haboob. "Glenda!" she yelled again, and she pointed to Chicaletta's shoulder.

Chicaletta lifted her right hand as if she were holding a trophy. Inside her grip was a bat with perfectly applied red lipstick and horn-rimmed goggles. Relief washed over Ali.

Alison Liv Isner pushed deeper into the sandstorm.

CHAPTER 4

They traveled for nearly a mile, post-holing in the soft sand. Ali's thighs burned, and her back ached from near falls. With limited visibility, she was forced to rely solely on the compass.

Then, out of nowhere, she kicked something hard. She crouched down, just inches away and saw a stone arm. Broken statues and collapsed pillars littered the ground. One statue was missing a hand, and its nose was chipped flat. The fallen hand gripped a large iron spear. The rust-brown surface was pocked with holes from the repeated beating of sand and wind.

"We must be close!" Ali shouted.

"It's about time," Tristan yelled from her belt. "My coat is filthy!"

Ali laughed. The fat rat looked ridiculous in his tiny goggles.

"This way," Chicaletta said.

Chicaletta untied herself from the rope, and Glenda once more gripped the hair on Chicaletta's shoulder. Glenda waved a leathery wing for everyone to follow with her.

Chicaletta led them to a perfectly cut rectangle in the side of a hidden building. It was blocked by a downed pillar. She nimbly climbed over it and disappeared into a tunnel.

Figgy was next. His hard hooves made it difficult to scramble over the pillar. After several attempts he backed up into the storm. Ali lost track of her four-legged friend until he burst through the dust, leaping like a leopard. He hee-hawed as he and Bait flew through the air, hurdling the pillar. She swore she could see a grin on Bait's face, showing razor-sharp teeth.

"I guess it's our turn, Tristan," Ali said.

"Good, get me out of this wretched storm."

Ali placed her hands on the pillar and swung

her legs over like a gymnast. Her feet hit the pillar, and it bounced her back. She fell flat on her back and tried to suck in air. With the wind knocked out of her, all she got was a mouth full of sand. Her lungs burned as she struggled to stand. Tristan said something to her, but she couldn't hear. Instead, she ducked under the pillar out of the storm.

"Human," Figgy said, "are you okay?"

"Yes," Ali said, coughing up sand.

"She fell pretty hard," Tristan said. "Someone should get her some water. She ate sand. I ate sand. We all ate sand. It was a sand feast."

Ali nodded, lifted an index finger, and erupted into another coughing fit.

Chicaletta rustled through the pack and produced a canteen. She unscrewed the lid and pressed it to Ali's lips.

Cold water rushed over Ali's lips and chin, dousing her white blouse. She swirled it in her mouth and spit it out. Now that her mouth was free of sand, she took a greedy drink.

"Thank you," Ali said, breathing heavy.

"Do you guys hear that?" Glenda asked.

"I feel it," Ali said.

Ali's feet vibrated against the ground as the low drums grew louder.

"The drums!" Ali yelled.

Chicaletta nodded, a small smile forming on her face. "As promised."

"I guess that means we're in the right spot?" Ali asked.

"Indeed," Bait agreed.

With the haboob raging just a few feet away from them the sky produced little light inside the tunnel. Sand swirled at their ankles. Chicaletta fumbled with a flint over a large copper pot lining the wall. A loud crackle, followed by a whoosh, started a succession of lit pots that lined the edge of the room. Ali had imagined the room much larger when it was dark, but now that it was lit, she saw it was only nine or ten feet deep.

"Wow," Ali said. She gently touched the rough, perfectly square stone walls.

The illuminated walls revealed intricate yet weathered symbols etched into the stone.

"What the heck is that supposed to mean?" Tristan asked.

"They're hieroglyphs," Bait said. "And they appear to be in incredible shape. Figs, take me a little closer, will you?"

Figgy's hooves clapped on the stone as he walked closer.

"Cool story," Tristan said. "But can you *read* them?"

"Actually," Bait lifted a fin, "see that fat one? Why, I believe that is one of your relatives, Tristan."

"I don't need this, this . . . abuse!" Tristan wiggled free from the loop on Ali's utility belt and scurried down her pant leg.

Ali laughed and shook her head. "Does anyone else know what this means?"

"Not everything is meant for our eyes," Chicaletta said. "Come, we must press forward. Figgy, perhaps you should shed the camp gear, but keep the small emergency pack." Chicaletta unhooked a strap, and it fell to the ground with a loud clang. A small one remained. "We will come back for it later. Let us see what we are up against this time."

"Wait!" Ali said. "Look—that one at the top." She pulled out the journal and opened it to the illustration of the headdress. "It's the all-seeing eye. We must be on the right track."

"Indeed," Chicaletta said. "Your mother was an excellent explorer and an even more prepared planner. Without her research, this could all be for naught."

Figgy shook his whole body like a dog shaking off water. Ali raised a hand while sand pelted the group.

"That feels much better." He folded his ears back.

Ali pet the wide dark spot on his head between his ears. His dirty white fur was thick and rough. The black hair around his eye looked less pronounced now that his hide was filthy.

She rested her hand on his back as they walked to the end of the room.

Glenda rustled through the camp gear on the ground and found nail polish and lipstick.

"This isn't some sort of gala, Glenda," Tristan said.

"It'll only take a second, Tristan," Glenda shot back. "I want to look good for the pharaoh." She quickly touched up her nails and lips, then tossed the beauty products back in the pack.

"He's dead," Tristan said. "Isn't he?"

Ali nodded.

Glenda glared at Tristan and said, "Next time you give me grief I'm gonna give you a big lipstick kiss on your head."

Tristan scurried away. "Uh, guys, look over here." Tristan pointed down past the edge of the room.

At the opposite edge of the room was a rectangular pool of water.

"Now what?" Glenda said. "This looks totally terrible."

"It must be at least a hundred feet wide and half as long," Ali said.

Chicaletta pushed a heavy copper pot near the edge, but it didn't illuminate the dark-green water much.

"I guess now is as good a time as any for me to go for a dip." Bait pulled his fins back as if he were stretching. "Ali, would you be a dear?" He pointed to his lid with a fin.

"Wait," she said. "Don't you need to see what type of water it is? I mean, can you breathe if it's salt water?"

"I'll be fine in any water. Except brackish." He shook his head, his jagged underbite even more pronounced. "I can't stand water that refuses to pick a side. It's uncivilized."

Ali unscrewed the lid from the jar, placing the leather covering in her pocket, and tilted it toward the water. Bait swam to the back of his jar and lunged forward with such force that he shot out like a cannonball. He landed with a very small splash.

He crested the surface for just a moment. "The water is splendid, darlings. I'll go have a look around. Toodles."

Waiting patiently, Ali looked around, hoping there was another way out. The pool of water appeared to extend out farther than the edges of the room, as if it went below the floor. An underwater tunnel, perhaps.

"What if we have to swim, Chicaletta?" Ali asked.

"Then we swim."

"But the journal," Ali said. "I don't want it to get ruined."

"Trust in your mother." Chicaletta rested a hand on Ali's back. "She was smart enough to use hearty paper and trusty ink. Keep it flat in your pocket, and do not disturb it until it is completely dry."

Ali's heart jumped. "Right, my mom. I—"

"I will tell you more about her when the time is right."

"Thank you." Ali bent at the waist and hugged

Chicaletta. Six years had passed since Ali's mother had died, and still the wounds felt fresh. While her memories were rich in detail, there weren't many. Burying her face in Chicaletta's silky golden locks, Ali felt her nerves calm, and her hands finally stopped shaking. She smelled a familiar scent she couldn't quite put her finger on. Regardless, it made her feel safe.

"Pardon me." Bait's British accent was suddenly thicker than normal. "I hate to interrupt, but I believe I've found a way."

"That's awesome," Glenda said. "Lead the way."

"Chicaletta, love, you're going to need the waterproof flashlights for this one." Bait went under to catch a breath, then emerged. "You're all going to have to hold your breath for about a minute."

Ali swallowed hard. She was a decent swimmer at best. Swimming lessons were for the rich, not her. The most she'd swum was with her friends at a shallow watering hole. Nothing like this.

"A minute?" Tristan groaned. "My lungs aren't that big. I can't hold it that long!"

"Then you're going to have to swim fast, lad," Bait said. "Head straight like you're heading for that wall, then dip under. Turn right at the fork. Then you'll be clear. Climb up on a platform to get out."

Tristan scurried to the edge, looked over his shoulder, and plopped in. He treaded water and said, "What? I want to get this sand out of my ear." He poked a pink finger into his ear.

Figgy entered next. He waded in slowly, then used all four legs to swim. He bobbed up and down wildly. Ali laughed at the spectacle. Figgy smiled back, a perfect ear-to-ear grin.

Glenda flew to the wall and fluttered down to the water and dipped a perfectly polished claw into the water. She flew back up and to the ledge.

"Chicaletta," Glenda said, "it's such a shame you have to get your hair wet."

"It will dry." Chicaletta grinned. "Are you comfortable swimming?"

"I'll manage," she said.

"And you?" Chicaletta turned to Ali.

"I'm . . ." She hesitated. "I will look within myself for strength."

"You have been listening," Chicaletta said. "I am impressed."

Ali neared the edge and took a deep breath. For the first time in her life, Alison Liv Isner literally took a leap of faith.

CHAPTER 5

The water was colder than she had thought it might be. As she entered, it took her breath away. Lightly touching her back pocket to ensure the journal was still firmly there, she took a deep breath. She treaded water until she encountered the overhanging wall. Her heavy, water-logged boots were cumbersome and weighed her down. Chicaletta and Glenda swam next to her until she was ready.

"When you are ready," Chicaletta handed her a waterproof flashlight, "go straight until you see the fork, turn right, and we will all be there. We must all go at our own pace."

Glenda sucked in a small, high-pitched breath and dive-bombed into the water, like a bird trying to catch its prey in the water. Chicaletta dove next. Ali followed. She filled her lungs with as much air as possible, placed her hands on the coarse sandstone wall and pushed down until she was under the wall.

Her flashlight only illuminated a small sliver in the dark green water. She could barely make out her friends in front of her. Figgy's four legs kicking wildly led the pack. Bait was correct. Within a few strokes she touched the wall and was forced to go left or right. As she turned to the right, something caught her eye in the beam of her flashlight. *It's just your imagination.* She swam, kicking as hard as she could. Then something bumped her.

She whipped around. A swirl of bubbles erupted and clouded her already limited vision. As the bubbles subsided, she moved her flashlight back and forth wildly until she landed on a white foot.

No, not a foot—a claw, wrapped in linen. Moving her flashlight up, she saw that the clawed foot was attached to a crocodile. A mummified crocodile. One of its legs was missing. The body was badly decayed. She wanted to scream but only produced bubbles. She'd only been under-water fifteen seconds, but her lungs already burned. Her eyes widened as she thrust her arms and legs forward, nearly bending herself in half in an attempt to propel her body backward.

Flailing about only brought attention to herself, and the mummified croc turned to face her. Its ribs were exposed on its left side, and despite the eyes being long gone, it somehow saw her and pursued her.

Still pushing backward, Ali bumped into Figgy's rump. She shifted to the side and kicked once more. Before she had a chance to point to the croc she felt a quick, hard pressure snap onto her leg. The burro's eyes grew wide; his lips pulled back, exposing clenched teeth.

Pointing her flashlight at the crocodile, she saw it had both her boot and Figgy's tail in its massive mummified jaws. Ali's heart raced. The sharp teeth sank into the leather of her boot. Her lungs protested for more air, and her ankle twisted. Coming to her senses, she used her free leg and kicked the croc in the mouth. The rotting mummy croc went in one direction, but its teeth and gums remained on Ali and Figgy.

Reaching down, she unhinged the clenched mouth and discarded it into the abyss below. Broken teeth drifted to the bottom. Fortunately, the old teeth hadn't punctured her skin. She turned to see if Figgy was okay but instead was greeted with the face of the toothless croc. This time she bashed it with the heel of her boot but immediately regretted it.

Alison Liv Isner realized the croc had captured a very pretty bat, with perfectly polished red nails, red lipstick, and the longest eyelashes she'd ever seen.

CHAPTER 6

Ali reached for her crossbow on her back and readied the weapon. Her flashlight tumbled to the depths below and landed on its handle, with the light shining up.

The crocodile seemed to sense this, and to Ali's horror, it rolled violently with Glenda in its mouth.

A death roll, Ali thought.

Ali brought the crossbow to her shoulder. The mummy croc was in her sights. She squeezed the trigger, and the arrow flung out of the bow. It slipped lazily through the water, but her aim was still good. It pierced the croc's side, and to Ali's astonishment, it went straight through, and the mummified crocodile was unfazed.

Figgy swam by and kicked the croc in the tail with his heavy hooves. Bone dust clouded the water. The tail fell off and fluttered to the bottom like a feather in the sky. Tristan swam by and fled to safety.

Ali's lungs seared in her chest. The remaining air she had stored escaped in a flurry of bubbles. Every last drop of oxygen in her lungs was gone.

In a last, desperate attempt Ali readied another arrow. Her hands shook. Relying on instinct, she released the arrow and shot it through the neck. The croc stopped swimming and turned toward Ali. Just then Chicaletta raised her machete high and sliced through the water and landed the blade on its neck, decapitating it. The head tumbled toward the depths.

Heart racing, lungs begging for air, Ali pulled her grappling-hook arrow and shot it into the side of the falling croc head, narrowly missing Glenda before it reached the bottom. Ali waved her hand at her friends toward the exit stone platform. She pulled on the rope as she ascended.

Bursting out of the water, Ali sucked in a deep breath and inadvertently swallowed some water in the process. She slapped her heavy arms onto the stone platform and army-crawled away from the edge. Chicaletta took the rope from her weak hand and pulled the croc head onto the platform. Chicaletta's normally fluffy, shiny golden hair was now matted to her thin gray body. Ali hadn't realized how small Chicaletta really was under all her hair.

"Did you guys see that mummy crocodile?" Tristan asked. Then he screamed. "Ah! Why did you bring it here?"

Ali coughed a few more times before scrambling over to the head of the crocodile. Chicaletta had already pulled Glenda free from its mouth. She lay there, lifeless, her leather wings plopped open on either side of her limp body.

Ali turned Glenda on her side and gently patted her back with her index finger. Glenda's small chest finally rose and showed life. The bat convulsed then turned to her side, spitting water from her mouth. The entire group let out a collective sigh and waited. Ali continued to gently stroke her little back.

Glenda gasped for air and coughed. They waited. A hitch caught in Ali's throat as tears welled in her eyes. Chicaletta interlaced her fingers with Ali's. She gripped Chicaletta's calloused hand back, thankful for her friend.

Finally, Glenda propped herself up with a sopping wing.

"Did I get him?" Glenda asked. "That ugly croc, did I get him?"

"Yes." Ali laughed, and a single tear rolled down her cheek. "You got him."

"Oh dang." Glenda examined her claw. "I chipped a nail."

Ali scooped her up and hugged her the best way she could. Still rattled, she released a pensive breath.

"You were very brave back there, Alison, just like your mother," Chicaletta said. "Eloise would have been proud."

Ali returned the compliment with a lopsided smile.

"Pardon me, but could I have a bit of assistance?" Bait said, splashing in the water.

"Oh, Bait!" Ali removed Bait's jar from Figgy's neck and rushed over to the edge. "I'm so sorry. We forgot."

"It's quite all right, love. Glenda was certainly the priority."

Ali scooped him into the jar and secured the lid.

"Ah yes, much better," Bait said.

Ali knelt and secured him around Figgy's neck. Then she took Figgy's muzzle in her hands and gently stroked it. "Figgy, how's your tail?"

"It's okay, human," he said. "The crocodile's teeth were too brittle to break my hide."

"Do you think we should go back?" Ali asked. "Forget this mission?"

"And risk running into another mummy croc?" Tristan said. "I'll take my chances going forward, thank you."

"But—" Ali said.

"Do you see this?" Tristan held up his perfectly pink tail. "People pay tens of dollars for a tail like this. Now, the last thing I'm going to do is risk a croc snapping it off."

"Of course, Tristan," Ali said. "It's a very nice tail."

"Very nice?" He tossed his tail to the ground. "Very nice? I—I'm speechless!" He threw his hands in the air.

"Yes, yes, Tristan, it's a fine tail indeed," Bait said. "Moving on to more pressing matters, the lass brings up a good point."

"But the Geese," Figgy said. "They could be right behind us or digging in from a different direction."

"Guys, I'm totally okay," Glenda said. "Nothing a little nail polish won't fix."

Everyone turned to Chicaletta.

"This mission is bigger than us," she said. "If the Geese find the headdress before us, it will have devastating consequences for the world.

They would have the most powerful tool on earth. If they can see the future, they can alter destiny. We must push on."

Ali nodded, stood, and walked forward. Everyone followed.

At only eleven years old, Alison Liv Isner had become a warrior for all humanity.

CHAPTER 7

They walked down a hallway in silence, save for the constant clippity-clop of Figgy's hooves. At the end of the hallway was a long, narrow room. Three-foot-high copper pots lined the room.

Glenda flew to the top of one of the pots. "Incense and oil," she said, sniffing the air.

"Tristan, fetch me the matches from Figgy's pack, please," Chicaletta said.

"Why me?" Tristan scowled but scurried up Figgy's leg and searched through the pack. "I have to do *everything* around here."

"Oh no!" Ali said. "Did they get wet?"

Chicaletta opened a plastic case and removed a match. "One must always prepare beforehand. This case is waterproof." She lit a match and flicked it into the top of one of the pots. Flames five feet high licked out of the top of the copper vessel.

"Light them all," Ali suggested.

Chicaletta worked quickly, striking matches and dropping them into every pot. A soft yellow glow lit up the room.

A pile of ropes, rags, and wooden barrels sat against one of the long walls at the opposite end. A few feet away was the real prize, a gigantic, sandstone, carved face. It resembled a giant pharaoh pushing his face through the wall, headdress and all.

The carving reminded Ali of Mount Rushmore. One summer, right before she lost her mom, her parents had taken her to the Black Hills of South Dakota. Because of her mom's incredible expeditions, they were invited to see the construction of the massive carving. George Washington was still under construction, and the three other presidents wouldn't grace the mountain for years. But even in its infancy, the monument was incredible to her.

"Wow," Ali said. "I've seen something like this before, with my parents."

"What is it?" Figgy asked. "Are those ruby eyes?"

"Let me look," Glenda said. She perched on Figgy's head between his ears. "Yes, they totally are. They must be the size of basketballs! Pretties!"

"Well, stay away from them." Tristan scoffed. "We don't need another 'pretty for the pretties' incident."

"I was enchanted," she said. "So not my fault at all."

"It really wasn't," Ali said. "The Temple of the Monkey God was full of booby traps and puzzles."

"It was not unlike this expedition," Chicaletta said. "One must always keep their wits about themselves and not fall prey to the tricks. Glenda's enchantment should remain a stark reminder for us all."

"Fine, fine," Tristan said. "I forgive you, Glenda."

Glenda's mouth fell agape.

"Forgive me for interrupting," Bait said, "but as Chicaletta mentioned, the Geese could be right behind us."

"What are we waiting for?" Figgy asked. "Let's go."

He stepped a hoof into the room, then another. Before Ali could step behind him, a three-foot-long pole with a flaming spear on each end shot out of each eye. One hit the wall, then landed on the ground, the flame fizzled out. The second angled toward them and narrowly missed Figgy's leg. Leaping back, he knocked down Ali. A long rope attached to the projectile reeled it back into the ruby eyes, then shot it out again, like a popgun Ali's dad sold for kids at the store.

"Get back!" Ali yelled, holding her arms out. "We don't want to get hit by those."

"Human, what do we do?" Figgy asked.

"I'm not sure," Ali said. "But we've got to do something. One came right for you. I'm not sure if they follow us or if it was just bad luck."

"Why go in there?" Glenda asked. "I didn't see an exit. You guys, I thought I was up for this, but now I'm not so sure."

Ali furrowed her brow. Glenda was right. There wasn't a clear way out.

"This pyramid," Chicaletta said, "is filled with secrets and puzzles, for the headdress is sacred and powerful and must be protected. Alison, please consult the journal."

"It's still wet." Ali pulled the journal from her pocket. "Is it safe to open?"

Chicaletta shook her head. Her beautiful, long hair, now almost dry, swished as she moved her head.

"Chicaletta's right," Ali said. "We have to press forward."

"Figaro, let me have another peek," Bait said. Figgy toed the threshold to the room. "What about that pile of rubbish we saw in the corner?

Could we run and hide behind it?"

"It is our best option," Chicaletta said. "Let us run. Right—now!"

She took off. Though she was a giant golden lion tamarin, she only stood roughly three feet tall. As she ran, she was a blur of hair as she zig-zagged in the room. Jumping over the long shaft attached to the spears and somersaulting toward the pile, she was an acrobat. Diving at the last minute behind the broken barrels, Ali looked on next to her friends as the spears shot out and retracted.

"Human," Figgy said. "You're next."

"We all go, together," Ali said. "Tristan," she turned to the fat rat, "want a ride?"

Before she could even finish her question, Tristan crawled up her leg and settled into her utility belt.

"Does this make us even?" she whispered to him.

"I guess." He crossed his arms. "As long as you get us there safely."

"It really *is* a nice tail." Ali laughed. "Ready?"

Ali snapped her fingers, and they all ran down the long, narrow room. The tall flames from the pots cast long, distorted shadows around the room. Figgy and Bait were the first to join Chicaletta behind the pile of equipment, then Ali with Tristan as her side arm. Glenda finally joined them as both flaming spears honed in on her.

"I smell burned hair," Ali said.

Figgy looked away, bashful.

"Oh, Figgy," Ali said. "You burned the top of your head." She gently touched the singed hair. "Are you okay? That was a close call!"

"I'm okay, human," Figgy said. "Just a little embarrassed. The spear went right between my ears!"

"One should not feel shame while sacrificing their own safety for the safety of the world," Chicaletta said. "You did well, Figgy."

The six adventurers huddled behind the pile of discarded ropes, barrels, linen, axes, hammers, and other random trash. Ali studied the spears as they hit the walls, clanked onto the ground, flame extinguished, then reeled back into the tear ducts of the eyes, like someone casting for fish.

"It seems like the spears have to recharge and relight," Ali said, shifting her weight from foot to foot. "I think that's why they return to the eyes for a moment. Look how slowly they're reeled back in, then they shoot out at full strength."

"I believe you're right, love," Bait said. "It also appears the angle of this trash precludes them from reaching us."

"That's a relief," Ali said. "But I'm not sure what to do now."

"Let me know what you guys come up with," Glenda said. She rummaged through the random pieces and posed in front of a broken mirror. "I need to examine my injuries."

"Glenda," Ali turned to her, "what did you find?"

"Oh no," Glenda said, ignoring Ali. "I'm a

mess. That mummy crocodile did a real number on me. My mascara is running down my face. Why didn't you guys tell me?"

"Glenda," Figgy said, "at least you're not missing any fur. Maybe you should put the mirror down."

"Please," Glenda cried. She placed a small hand over her face, her wing shielding her body. "Take it away. I can't bear to look at myself another minute."

"I have an idea," Ali said. "No, a plan! Chicaletta, may I borrow your machete?"

Chicaletta slowly nodded and handed her the sharp blade from her leather shoulder strap.

"I'm outta here," Tristan said, then jumped free of Ali's utility belt.

Swallowing a big spoonful of trepidation, Ali said, "Wish me luck."

"Human," Figgy said, "what are you doing?"

"I'm looking within myself," Ali turned to Chicaletta, "to find a solution."

Chicaletta nodded once more.

Ali's heart rate quickened, and her breath became shallow. She peaked around the barrel, waiting for the spears to shoot out of the ruby eyes. The first one hit the ceiling and bounced onto the ground with a loud clank. The second one whizzed right past Ali's face, and the heat from the flame took her breath away.

"Look out!" Glenda screamed.

Alison Liv Isner raised Chicaletta's machete and hoped for the best.

CHAPTER 8

Ali brought the blade down with as much force as she could muster on the rope attached to the spear. The rope was thicker than she'd realized. Her hands vibrated up to her arms from the impact. It was the same way her hands hurt after striking a baseball with a wooden bat.

The rope was only half severed. She wiggled the sharp blade back and forth to free it. Then the rope slowly retracted. She lifted the machete high once more, ran toward the initial cut, and brought the blade down. The rope slithered back up to the eye, leaving the spear on the ground.

"Yes!" Ali yelled. She picked up the hot spear, then dropped it, shaking her hands. "Ouch!"

"Come back," Glenda yelled. "The other spear

is already back in the eye!"

"Just give me one second!" Ali yelled. "I can do this."

Ali untucked her shirt and ripped a piece of material free at the bottom. Sweat dotted her brow. She wrapped it around the spear and ran toward the stone face. She threw it at the ruby eye. Intense heat and light glowed within the ruby eye just before it exploded into small bits. Shiny shards of the red gemstone rained down on the room.

Cheers erupted from her friends.

"Do that again so we can get out of here," Tristan said, scratching his belly.

Stepping back, Ali readied herself for the remaining spear. But this one, renewed with power from the eye, bounced toward her with angry authority. Stumbling over her boots, Ali headed back toward the barrels again.

"Shoot," she mumbled.

She caught herself and landed on her hands and knees. Ali sprang to her feet and sprinted toward her friends.

"That was totally awesome," Glenda said.

"I'm not done yet." Ali panted.

"Glenda's right," Bait said. "It was brilliant."

"But," Ali said, lifting her chin, "I only got one of the spears."

"One must not focus on what has not been done," Chicaletta said, cupping Ali's chin, "but rather, what one has accomplished. Take credit where it is due."

"Thank you." Ali's voice caught in her throat.

"Now go back out," Chicaletta said, "with your head held high, and disarm the other eye. Now is not the time to second guess oneself."

Ali stood with firm posture and ran out into the open. Watching the eye, she waited for the spear once again. She had to hurry; the Geese could be right behind them. Chicaletta was right: it was time to be brave.

The fire spear zipped across the room at lightning speed, right at her. She waited until the last second, then dodged out of the way. This time she was ready and brought down the machete with as much force as she could muster. Sparks erupted when the blade struck the stone floor, but the rope severed and wiggled back into the eye.

Ali ran to the fallen spear. It still smoked. She kicked it with her boot; heat radiated through the leather. *There's no time to wait for it to cool!* Blinking hard, she whispered "Mom" to herself.

A smile formed on Ali's lips. She pulled an arrow from her quiver and loaded her crossbow. She aimed at the remaining eye and released the arrow.

The ruby exploded with a violent force. Red shards rained down. Her friends cheered and emerged from their hiding place. Chicaletta clapped. Ali walked toward the pharaoh and met her friends at the base of the stone face. Two hollow black eyes loomed above them.

"It worked!" Ali said. "Why didn't I think of that before?"

"Disarming them first was a better idea,"

Chicaletta said. "A solid plan indeed."

"Now what?" She panted. "I guess I expected a secret door to open or something."

Chicaletta nimbly climbed onto the stone lip. "Sometimes a door does not look like a door." She stuck her head into the empty eye sockets above them. "But more like a window."

She pulled herself up and did a backflip off the face. As she rotated, she kicked her legs out, making contact with the face. Stone crumbled down, and a large hole appeared where the eye had been. Soft yellow light from behind the eye now illuminated the room.

Tristan flinched and ducked behind Ali's calf. "Not another flaming spear! I don't want to be shish kebabbed today."

Chicaletta disappeared behind the face, and she beckoned them to follow. "It is not. It is just flame light. Come with me."

Alison Liv Isner climbed through the mask, stepped onto the crumbling platform, and gasped.

CHAPTER 9

Ali looked down at the large stone platform. Her stomach churned. The platform was barely attached to the wall, jutting out into midair. To her left was another small beginning of a stairway protruding out from the circular room. Looking up, Ali realized the room was a tall cylinder, and the crumbling stairway was the only way forward.

A disintegrating ceiling allowed a small amount of light and sand from the raging haboob to illuminate the lofty circular room. Ali clicked on her flashlight and pointed it down. She saw one step, but that was the furthest her light cast. Pointing toward the top, she had a better view. She gauged the steps. They varied between one foot and a couple feet apart. There were at least twenty or more wrapped around the sides of the room.

"Up?" Ali asked.

"Figs," Bait said, "will you be able to make the step?"

"I think so." He padded toward the edge and stared forward.

"Figgy," Ali said. "I'm so sorry. I didn't even think about that."

"It's okay, human."

"How about I go last?" Ali petted the soft spot between his ears. The singed hair tickled her fingertips. "Then as long as you can get your front feet, er, hooves, on the step in front, I can push you from behind."

"Brilliant, love," Bait said.

Until that moment, it hadn't even occurred to Ali that Bait depended on this plan as much as Figgy.

"Tristan—" Ali held out the loop on her belt. "You want a ride?"

"And risk having Figgy pull me down?" he asked. "No thanks. I'll take my chances on my own." The rat began to stretch. "Gotta get limber."

Tristan leaped onto the first step. The moment his little feet touched the steps a loud scraping sound drew their attention to him. The stair on which the rat stood slowly retracted into the wall.

"Work swiftly and stay together," Chicaletta said. "Tristan, do not jump ahead until we are all firmly on the same step."

"Fine." He crossed his arms and sat on his fat bottom.

"I'll hover above," Glenda said. "Don't worry about me. You'll need the extra room on each step."

Chicaletta jumped, quickly turned, and held her arms out for Figgy.

"Will we all fit?" Ali asked.

"It is larger than it looks. You must hurry."

Figgy cautiously reached one hoof out, and it landed on the unstable stone. His other front leg followed. Ali felt his back legs shaking. She wasn't sure if it was from fear or just the instability.

"On three," Ali said. "One, two, three!" She pushed as Figgy did his best to propel himself up and forward onto the next platform. His back hooves slipped, but Ali managed to keep him moving forward. "Oh no!" she yelled. She waved her arms in large circles behind her to regain her balance.

Running and jumping with all her might, she landed on the crowded step with her friends. The stone made a terrible scraping noise, like nails on a blackboard.

The step was slowly getting sucked into the wall.

Shivers fell down Ali's spine.

"Now," Chicaletta said to Tristan.

"Wait!" Glenda yelled. "Look down!"

Ali gasped. Six Geese walked into the room only a few steps below.

"Hurry!" Chicaletta said. "There is not a moment to waste."

Figgy brayed.

Chicaletta pulled on the front of Figgy while Ali pushed him from behind. Once he was firmly on, Ali jumped onto the next step.

Chicaletta jumped a moment after Tristan. As predicted, the new stair performed the same disappearing act as the last one. They struggled to get Figgy on safely, Chicaletta helping from the front, Ali pushing from behind, but they persevered.

"Again," Chicaletta said.

"Where are the Geese?" Bait asked.

"Let me look," Glenda said, flying over them. "Oh no! They're shooting grappling arrows to the wall, trying to figure out a way up."

"Push!" Ali yelled to herself. The exhausted donkey felt heavier with each step.

They implemented this same routine over and over. They moved so quickly Ali became dizzy as they made their way up and around the room. Her head throbbed, and sweat pooled around her neck. Finally, they saw a door just five stairs way. Figgy's entire body quivered on the last few steps. His footing was messy and hesitant. Ali wasn't sure if it was exhaustion, the Geese, or nerves. Either way, she was grateful for the landing.

"Just a few more steps," Glenda said. "You can totally do it."

The beautiful bat's sparkle in her eyes was replaced with fatigue.

"Good," Tristan said. "I'm tired of waiting on these slow-pokes."

"How are you doing, Figgy?" Glenda squeaked.

He grunted and huffed a few times, but no real words escaped his mouth. Ali furrowed her brow and hoped he could hold on for a few more minutes.

"We're almost there." Ali heaved Figgy up another step. His backside had become slick with perspiration. She grabbed onto the stone wall for support. "Al . . . most there."

Tristan was the first onto the upper platform

with the door. He lay on his side and propped his head up with his fist, like a Greek god waiting for someone to feed him grapes. Glenda landed next to him and let out a tiny but tired breath. Chicaletta was next, holding her arms out for Figgy. Then Figgy, completely exhausted, plopped one heavy hoof onto the stone, then the next. Ali nearly toppled over. He'd given up, and his weight was solely on Ali.

"Come on, Figgy." Ali grunted. The stair she stood on slid halfway into the wall. "I need your help."

A labored and wet snort was his answer.

"Figs," Bait said. "You've been my best mate for years." The stone was not only disappearing into the wall, but also starting to crumble. "You won't be my friend for another ten years if you can't make it up this last step."

Figgy's back hoof slipped on the slick stone.

"If you can't do it for your chap, do it for the lass. She's slipping!"

His weight shifted under Ali's hands. It felt

lighter to her.

"Human!" he grunted.

With a final push, he was on the platform and collapsed. Bait's jar clanked as it hit the rock floor.

The stone groaned under Ali's feet. Left with no other choice, she jumped off balance. Immediately, she knew it wasn't a strong enough jump. She thrust her arms forward, hoping to grab onto the landing.

Chicaletta reached for her. The monkey's calloused hand gripped her outstretched arms. With incredible strength she pulled Ali safely onto the platform. Then Chicaletta pushed a protruding stone and the door scraped open.

Ali flinched. The sound reminded her of the stairs that just disappeared.

She crawled on her hands and knees, past the open door, and into a long hallway. The hall floor was covered in sand. She lay on the cold sand, next to an exhausted burro with a fish around his neck in a mason jar. Ali stared at the jar for a moment, relieved it hadn't broken on impact. The cold from the sand seeped through her ripped white shirt and into her skin. Her tense muscles relaxed.

"Finally," Tristan said. "You guys took forever."

Alison Liv Isner laughed hysterically.

CHAPTER 10

"Where are we?" Ali asked once she regained her composure.

"Are you okay, human?" Figgy asked.

"Am I okay?" She laughed again. "Figgy! I should be asking you that question."

"Perhaps we should stop for a moment," Bait said. "Maybe for a spot of water?"

"What about the Geese?" Ali asked.

"The door is locked," Chicaletta said. "It will hold them off a little longer if they are able to climb up here. But we must rest for a moment, so we are at our best."

Everyone agreed. Chicaletta and Ali drank from canteens stashed in Figgy's emergency pack. Ali poured water into a dish for the rest to drink, save for Bait. Figgy's ears perked back up, Chicaletta eye's brightened, Tristan seemed to be unaffected, and color returned to Glenda's lip. Although, Ali was certain she'd just reapplied her lipstick.

"Shall we?" Bait asked.

The long hallway was lined with the same copper pots they'd seen before. Some were lit, others not. Sand covered the stone floor, cushioning Ali's tired feet.

Tristan sighed.

"How high up do you think we've climbed?" Ali asked.

"If I had to guess," Chicaletta said, "I would say we are just below the middle of the pyramid."

"This place is super neat," Glenda said.

"It feels odd," Ali said. The hair on her arms stood at attention, rubbing against the long sleeves of her thin shirt. "Something about it feels weird to me. Maybe we should whisper, not draw attention to ourselves."

"Yes," Chicaletta agreed. "The Geese are on

our trail."

Tristan fell.

"Who tripped me?" he asked.

"What the—" Figgy echoed. "Tristan, did you just bite my leg?"

"Excuse me!" Tristan yelled. "Me? Rats do not eat burros, thank you very much. And furthermore—"

"Ouch!" Figgy yelled.

"The ground," Tristan scrambled to his feet and up Ali's pant leg, burrowing firmly into her belt, "it's moving."

Ali gently stroked Tristan's soft head, then bent to examine the sand. After reaching for the sand, she gasped and quickly pulled her hand back as if she'd touched fire.

"Scorpions! They're coming up from the ground."

"Run," Chicaletta said. "The pots will be our sanctuary."

Ali found one without a flame nearby and clambered on to it. The opening was covered with a soft wax, but it held her weight. But she balanced on the wide copper edges just in case. Figgy took a few steps back, then with a short trot jumped onto the pot like a circus animal jumping onto a barrel. He balanced precariously atop one next to her. Chicaletta, with a bat clinging to her shoulder, sat atop the next pot down from her.

"Now what?" Tristan asked.

He was right. This wasn't a plan, not a good one anyway. Thousands of black scorpions emerged from the sand and were inching their way to the pots.

"What's that smell?" Tristan sniffed the air. His whiskers glistened in the low light. "It's familiar."

"Not now, lad," Bait shouted. "We have real pressing matters."

"I know this smell," he said, sniffing the air. "It's sweet, maybe a hint of vanilla."

"What are we going to do?" Ali's eyes welled with tears. Scorpions crawled over the bases of the pots, covering them like thick, black syrup. "The journal is still damp. There's no way I can see what my mom would do."

"Maybe a touch of nuttiness too?" Tristan interrupted, sniffing the air again. "Yes, it definitely has a touch of nuttiness."

"Tristan, that is enough!" Chicaletta said.

"It's—" Tristan wiggled out of Ali's belt and onto the rim of the pot. He scratched at the center of the pot, then sunk his teeth into the thick wax. Rearing back, he spit a chunk of it onto the ground. Then he reached a pink hand in, pulled it back and licked it. "Honey! I knew it. This is high-grade stuff, not the clove honey. *Real* honey." He dipped his hand back in for another taste. "It's delicious."

"Brilliant," Bait said, his British accent thick with sarcasm.

"I'm glad you have a snack." Figgy wobbled and almost fell into the sea of scorpions.

"I'm glad too." Tristan balanced over the edge, lapping up the honey. "Oh yeah, this stuff is great." He dipped his hand in over and over. The sticky gold honey coated his hairy arm up to his elbow.

"Yes," Chicaletta said. "That is it. The honey will buy us some time. Everyone, check your pots, break the wax seal, and scoop it out. Throw it onto the scorpions. It should impede their progress. Glenda, please see if you can scout out an exit."

She batted her long lashes at Chicaletta and fluttered off.

Ali looked from side to side, unsure of the plan.

"And waste it?" Tristan gasped. "Never. It's too glorious and tasty! Just look at how much honey there is. I could live in this pyramid forever."

They ignored his protests and dipped their hands and scooped out the honey. Figgy resorted to kicking at it with a hoof. It splashed in big waves over the side. The sticky scorpions embodied an expression Ali had heard her grandmother use: they were moving like molasses in January. But it wasn't enough. It would keep the scorpions at bay for a few minutes, but they greatly outnumbered them.

"Hey," Glenda fluttered between them, "there's an opening directly above us."

"What is up there?" Chicaletta asked.

"It was weird," she said. "Like, super weird. It was smelly, for one. But more importantly, there were a whole bunch of columns in the room. Big ones, all varying in height but wide enough to stand."

"Any scorpions or crocs?" Figgy asked.

"Nope," she said.

"Sounds good to me." Ali pulled her grapple arrow out of her quiver. "I'll go first."

"Don't forget me." Tristan's hair was matted down slick, covered in honey. He scurried up her leg but got stuck trying to wiggle into the belt.

"How could anyone forget about you?" Ali tried to help him into the belt but only succeeded in tearing out a bit of hair.

"Ouch!" Tristan screamed. "Careful, this is the only coat I've got."

"What about Figgy?" Ali asked. "How will we get him and Bait up there?"

Figgy fixed his gaze to the ground.

"You two go first," Chicaletta said to Ali. "I will tie Figgy to the rope so he is secure, then climb up the rope. We will all work together to pull him and Bait up."

"Hurry," Glenda squeaked. "The scorpions are getting meaner."

The arachnids were stinging each other and stuck in clumps of honey.

Ali shot high above, hoping the grappling-hook arrow would catch the sandstone edge on her first try. It went high and straight. Her heart sank as she saw it careening back down toward the sand. It landed with a sickening crack on top of a heap of scorpions. Pale-yellow innards from squished scorpions spilled out of hundreds of bugs.

"Shoot," Ali said, pulling the rope back.

"Alison," Chicaletta said, "you have the skills to do this."

Ali nodded and took a calming breath. *Look within yourself for strength.*

She flicked smashed scorpions and yellow guts from the arrow. The smell of arachnid guts was sharp. She wrinkled her nose, then gagged on the scent.

She readied her arrow again and shot it. The archery lessons had paid off; she felt the tension as it sank into something high above. She gave the rope two sharp jerks to make sure it was secure. Wrapping her leg around the long rope attached to the grapple, she pulled herself up. She raised her legs and cinched the rope between her knees. Her forearms burned, and her breath came in short bursts as she pulled herself up.

Just as Glenda had promised, she smelled the room before she arrived. Her nose was greeted with the offending smell of thick ammonia. As she crested the edge, she steadied her hands on either side and pulled herself up. The hole looked intentional. It was a perfect circle, roughly four feet wide.

"I'm up, Chicaletta," Ali yelled down.

Ali checked the arrow to make sure it was still secure in the wall. She felt all the slack pulled tight. Figgy's weight tested the strength of the rope. Before she could ask, Chicaletta emerged over the edge. The monkey easily scaled the rope with Glenda on her shoulder. It was funny to Ali; she'd heard of pirates with parrots, but never a giant golden lion tamarin with a lipstick-wearing bat on her shoulder.

"You ready, Figgy? Bait?" Ali shouted.

He grunted. Bait bubbled in his jar.

Everyone but Glenda grabbed hold of the rope. They lined up like they were playing tug of war. As slow going as the process seemed, the tension on the rope was fierce. No one said anything. As they pulled, the rope rubbed against the sandstone lip. Ali focused her attention on it. If the rope frayed, that would be the end of Figgy and Bait.

"Pull!" Chicaletta commanded.

Ali's shoulders strained, but she did as she was told. She pulled as hard as she could, then took a small step back, confirming their progress.

"Again," Chicaletta said. "Pull!"

"Lay off the cheeseburgers, Figgy," Tristan yelled. "He's too heavy!"

"No," Ali said, her voice strained. "He's perfect. Pull, Tristan, I know you can do it. You're stronger than you think."

Her forearms cramped.

Glenda flew up from the abyss. "He's close, but you guys need to hurry. The rope is starting to dig in to Figgy's sides."

"See?" Tristan shook his head. "I told you. Cheeseburgers. And you guys think *I'm* fat."

"Not now, chap," Bait yelled from below the edge.

"Look within yourself for strength. Do not give up," Chicaletta said.

They finally had the donkey even with the hole. He placed his front hooves on the edge, and they yanked him one final time. Figgy hee-hawed, and it echoed in the cavernous room.

"Thank you," Figgy said. "I'm sorry I've been such a pain."

"If you're a pain, Figs," Bait said, "then what does that make me, old pal? Why, I couldn't get around without you."

"You're my best friend." Figgy shuffled his front hooves.

"And you're mine," Bait said. "We're all friends. That's what we're for."

"Bait is correct," Chicaletta said. "We are all useful when the moment presents," she said, nodding to Ali. "We all possess separate yet equally important talents. We are better together."

Ali kneeled and took Bait's jar in one hand and the back of Figgy's head in the other. She nuzzled her face against his. Chicaletta placed a calloused hand on her back, Glenda landed on Ali's shoulder, and Tristan placed a tiny finger on Figgy's hoof.

They were silent for a few moments.

"We really *are* better together," Ali said.

Tristan farted.

Ali waved a hand in front of her nose. "Okay then." She stood, walked around the hole, and peered into the room. "Let's figure this room out."

Alison Liv Isner slipped on a puddle of a putrid, white mystery substance.

CHAPTER 11

Ali quickly stood and tried to rid herself of the smelly, slimy substance. As she flung it off, her lungs filled with the acrid smell.

"What is this?" she asked.

"Hey," Glenda squeaked, "look up."

Dozens of columns, as high as fifty feet and as short as two feet, stood before them. Ali couldn't discern a pattern between them. Some were mere inches apart, others several feet. Stone platforms adorned the top of each column as if inviting them to test out their sturdiness. The room narrowed toward the top, and the source of their light was discovered.

"Blimey," Bait said. "We're in the center of the pyramid. We must be close."

"Hang on," Ali said. She ran back to the hole and removed her grapple arrow from the rock. "Just in case we need it again."

The first platform was only a few inches away, and she stepped onto it. She walked to the edge and stomped her foot. "It seems pretty solid."

Figgy's hooves clip-clopped on the smooth rock. Chicaletta was next, followed by Tristan and Glenda, who walked after she flew over the small gap.

The next one was two feet away and four feet down. Ali's heart fluttered. Her hands shook. She sucked in a breath as if she were jumping into water. After leaping, she landed on the wobbly platform, and her knees buckled.

"This one isn't that stable." Her hands still shook from the adrenaline rush. "Figgy, I think you should come last so we can all use our weight to counter the opposite side."

Before Tristan could protest, Chicaletta scooped him up and leaped nimbly onto the lower column. Ali smiled at the monkey; her agility was certainly her strength. Glenda glided down.

"Hey." Tristan scowled. "I could have done it on my own. Besides," he pointed at Ali, "that's *her* job."

"Tristan," Ali said. "If you'd like a ride, get in my belt now. Otherwise, come over here. Everyone, come to the far edge."

Chicaletta was the last to approach the edge and waved everyone a few feet forward.

"If we are too close, we will all be bucked off when Figgy lands," she said. "Figgy," she said, nodding in his direction.

From their vantage point they could only see the edge of the tall platform, but they could hear his hooves racing across the stone. Then nothing. Ali stared at the small burro flying in the air at them. He landed with a thud. The entire platform shifted like water in a bumped fish tank. It swayed back and forth until it finally settled.

"My heavens," Bait said. "That smell, it seems to be getting stronger the lower we go."

Ali peered over the edge. "There are a lot of piles of that white gunk below."

"Too bad the next platforms aren't up," Glenda said.

The next three columns were close and spaced easily apart, almost as if they were a staircase. Four platforms later, they were only three feet off the ground.

Whoosh, whoosh, whoosh.

"What is that noise?" Ali asked. "It sounds like—like a fan."

Ali looked toward the hole-mottled ceiling. Before she had a clear view, instinct kicked in, and she ducked. Whatever made that noise had swooped down and nearly hit her. She wobbled for a moment before it swooped her again.

"Ah," Ali yelled.

Her arms stretched straight out, and she waved them in large circles to regain her balance. But it was useless. She fell off the platform and landed in a large pile of the white goop. Standing quickly, she tried to flick it off her arms, hands, and legs. The goo was dark-green and purple, with white streaks.

"Gross!" Ali said. "It stinks! Get it off me!" She started gagging. The goop matted her hair and threatened to land in her mouth.

Chicaletta and Figgy didn't have much luck either. They plummeted off the platform and landed in their own respective piles.

"What the heck was that thing?" Tristan leaned over the platform, yelling down to his friends.

"I'm not sure," Ali said, wading to the edge of the goop.

"What is this stuff?" Figgy flicked his hoof.

Glenda fluttered down toward them. "That—"

"No," Tristan interrupted. "Let me tell them." He laughed, slapping his knee. "Ha ha...let me...wait." He rolled onto his back in a fit of laughter.

"Tristan," Glenda said. "It's totally not funny. Not funny at all."

"You're right, it's *hilarious*! What you are covered in is," he said, then leaned back over the edge, facing them, "one hundred percent, grade A bird poop!" He again rolled onto his back, laughing. "Bird poop!"

"Ugh," Ali groaned. "We gotta get it off."

She tried shaking like a wet dog, but it was no use. Her backside and arms were covered in the feces.

"Ha ha!" Tristan pointed at them. He paused only for a moment; Ali's eyes had grown wide. "What?" he asked. "It's not like *I* made the stuff."

"Tristan!" Ali yelled. "Look out!"

Before he could respond, an enormous bird the size of an elephant snatched Tristan in its talons. It paused for a moment, locking eyes with Ali. The obsidian-black eyes looked cold and dead, and its wings were teal, the tips dark blue. Save for the red markings, the bird was various shades of brilliant blues.

"No, no, no," Ali mumbled quietly to herself. "No, this can't be happening!"

Laser focused, she ran to the nearest pillar and pulled herself up.

"Wait," Glenda said to Ali. "I can fly up there and get him."

"Can you carry him that long, love?" Bait asked.

"As long as he doesn't squirm too much," she said.

"Glenda, no. I don't want you to get captured," Ali said. "If the bird fights back, I have my crossbow. It's too dangerous for you."

"Human." Figgy trotted over to her. "What are you doing?"

"I'm," Ali said, turning to Chicaletta, "sacrificing myself for the greater good."

Chicaletta nodded at Ali.

"Besides," Ali continued, "I'm the only one Tristan will listen to."

"Isn't that the truth," Glenda said. "Okay, but I'll be watching in case I need to fly up and help."

"Good luck, human," Figgy said, his voice dropped.

"Oh, Figs," Bait said. "It'll be all right, mate, I promise. Right, lass?"

"Right," Ali grunted as she jumped up to the next platform.

She placed her palms on the stone surface and climbed up platform after platform until her heart skipped a beat. Perched over a massive nest in the top corner of the room were the giant bird and Tristan.

She climbed faster, shooting her arrow into a platform fifteen feet above her. After pulling on it to test its connection, she wrapped her poo-covered leg around it and climbed. Breathing heavily, she yanked the arrow from the post with raw hands and continued toward Tristan.

Suddenly, the bird spread its wings and dove toward her. As it approached, screams and cheers from below redirected the bird's attention. Chicaletta, Glenda, Figgy, and Bait all screamed, yelled, and waved their arms in a bid to distract it. Ali lay flat on the stone until she was sure she was out of its sight. When she had bounced back to her feet, she skipped over six more forms until she was at the edge of the thorny nest.

Alison Liv Isner peered over the edge of the nest, bracing herself for what she might see.

CHAPTER 12

Snuggly sound in a half-broken egg shell was Tristan the rat. The nest itself was the size of the storage room back at her father's shop. For a moment, Ali studied his unmoving body and wondered if he was dead. She reached out and gingerly touched his soft fur.

"Jingle jangle," he mumbled and rolled over.

"Tristan?" Ali whispered. "Jingle what?"

"It means let me sleep." He blinked hard a few times.

"Tristan," Ali sighed. "Get up. What are you doing?"

"Obviously I was napping." He rolled flat onto his back. "The operative word is *was*."

"Get up," Ali pleaded. "We have to go. The

gang is distracting the bird for now. We don't have much time."

"Later." Tristan stretched his arms above his head and yawned. "She's bringing me lunch."

"Lunch? What are you talking about? How do you know she doesn't think *you're* lunch?"

"I am not some common rodent, thank you very much." He jolted up. With hands on his hips, he shifted his eyes up and to the left. "I'll have you know, she thinks I'm her baby. And why wouldn't she? I'm adorable. Oh no." He jumped and looked over Ali's shoulder. "She's coming back. Hide!"

Ali looked behind her. She sucked in a sharp breath. The bird's colorful wings flapped swiftly, propelling itself toward them. Ali ducked behind the opposite side of the nest, balancing precariously on a stony edge.

The bird cooed at Tristan and lightly pecked him.

"Welcome back, Mother." Tristan held out his arms. "I see you've brought me a delicious worm."

The bird perched on the thick edge of the nest. Ali wondered where the beast had found a worm. She watched as it gobbled it up right in front of Tristan. Then it hit her, she remembered how birds feed their young. She covered her mouth, stifling a laugh. Tristan wasn't going to like this.

"What are you doing?" Tristan asked the bird. "What a cruel trick, to bring a worm and eat it right in front of me."

The bird tucked its neck down, then raised it back up three or four times. Then it pointed its beak directly at Tristan's mouth. Tristan screamed as the bird barfed worm all over him.

"Ah!" he screamed. "Why would you do that, Mother?" He flicked pieces of chewed-up worm off of his fur.

Satisfied with its work, the bird softly brushed its enormous wing over Tristan's back, then flew away. Ali guessed it was looking for more food to feed her "baby."

"Let's go." Ali reached for him, then thought

better of it.

"What's the point?" Tristan dramatically fell onto his back. "You're covered in poop, I'm covered in vomit. Life has lost its meaning."

"Tristan, if you think this is bad," she said, flapping her arms, "what's going to happen when it tries to teach you to fly? You know, kicks you out of the nest."

He shook from his head to tail, splattering puke everywhere. "Welp," he said, stepping onto the edge, "time to go."

Ali jumped down and onto the next platform. Tristan followed. Oddly, he didn't want a ride in Ali's belt, and she was thankful for that. They'd made it halfway down before the bird returned to its empty nest. It squawked. The ear-piercing noise shook the room. Ali felt the sound reverberate in the pit of her stomach.

"Oh no," Ali said. "Hurry!"

The fowl squawked, then swooped at them. Ali fell onto the platform and stayed as still as possible. A sense of sadness filled Ali. The bird sounded heartbroken. Ali was taking what it thought was its baby.

As she got closer to the bottom, the columns were spaced farther apart. Forced to shoot her grappling-hook arrow into the lower platform, she swung down and did her best to avoid running straight into the support system of the column. By now, Tristan had grown tired and was firmly in Ali's belt. Puke, honey and all. With each jump she swung like Tarzan. Her heart skipped a beat until they were on the next platform.

I hope my rope holds.

The bird stopped chasing them. Then the saddest squawk Ali had ever heard echoed through the large birdcage chamber. Her platform shook.

"Ali." Glenda flew erratically near her. "We found an exit."

"Where?" Ali's chest heaved as she balanced on a sandstone column.

"In that corner." Glenda batted her long lashes toward the opposite side of the pyramid. "We found a false wall. It's a little smaller than you, but I think you'll totally fit."

Ali paused on a platform, resting her hands on her knees. In the corner Chicaletta waved her arms.

"I see it," Ali said. "Go, take Tristan. I'll meet you there." She pulled the sticky, stinky rat from her belt. Glenda grasped him gently.

"Hey, I'm no piece of meat." Tristan hung limply from Glenda's grasp. "And watch the fur this time."

Glenda rolled her eyes and flew off with Tristan.

Ali swung down another few feet on her rope. *Thwup, thwup, thwup.*

Ali saw a shadow encompass her. Before she could react, the giant bird had snipped her rope with its formidable beak.

Alison Liv Isner plunged to the ground.

CHAPTER 13

Too terrified to scream, she squeezed her eyes shut and braced herself for the landing. Soft, smelly white poop broke her fall. She shook her head and jumped to her feet. Just then the iron grapple hook plopped into the bird poop next to her. She retrieved it. Chicaletta still waved her arms near a small hole, no more than four feet high.

The bird squawked. "I'm coming," Ali yelled to Chicaletta.

Running proved to be difficult. Not just because of the fear creeping at her psyche, but also because her boots were covered in slippery goo. The bird swooped at her once more. Ali ducked next to a pillar with a low platform, knowing the bird was too big to get close. She pressed her face against the cold, rough stone and gasped.

As the bird flew above to regain speed to dive-bomb again, Ali bolted toward her friends. Legs burning, arms weak from climbing, she pressed forward. She screamed as she heard the *thwup* of the wings approaching. It was so close.

Figgy burst through the opening. Ali tumbled to the ground. He reared up and kicked the bird as it swooped down. Ali rolled, jumped through the hole, tripped, landed on her back, and stared at the opening. Her chest rose and fell heavily as she caught her breath. A thick, two-foot talon wildly slashed as Figgy ran through the hole, barely escaping its grasp.

"Is everyone here?" Ali asked. "Did Glenda bring Tristan?"

"Yes." Tristan crawled near her head. "And I'll have you know she ripped out another chunk of my hair." He bent toward her ear. "I know she's just jealous of my luxurious coat. I've said it before, I'll say it a million times," he whispered.

"A simple thank you would suffice," Glenda called out. "I chipped two nails saving you!"

Ali still panted. She concentrated on a crack in the stone ceiling to calm her breath.

"If the scorpions do not stop the Geese, the bird certainly will," Chicaletta said. "We have overcome many obstacles and thwarted the Geese. You should be proud."

Ali smiled, and her face reddened.

"Love," Bait said, "I'm thrilled you're here and all, and know this is difficult for me to say. But would you mind taking a dip in the reflection pond? You're a touch ripe."

"Reflection pond?"

"Here," Glenda said. "Follow me. I'm not sure why Bait keeps calling it that. Must be a British thing."

Just two feet away was a perfect rectangle of water, no bigger than a large kitchen table. It was full to the brim, and new water circulated in while the old water flowed out over rocks. It was a rudimentary filter, but it seemed to work. All her friends had rinsed off in it, and yet the water was crystal clear.

Ali was silent. She pulled her mom's journal from her pocket. It hadn't gotten any bird poop on it, but it was still damp. Carefully placing it on the ground, she stepped down into the water. It was the perfect temperature. White goo streaked with purple and teal became a ring around her, clouding the water. She swished backward and leaned her head back. Dipping her long braids into the water, she clenched her eyes shut, then dipped her entire head. When she resurfaced, she felt energized. As if the water had healing properties. Blinking the water out of her eyes, she was amazed. The water was once again clear.

Chicaletta pulled the waterproof case from Figgy's pack. She removed a match and lit a pot against a wall. This single action caused a chain reaction. When one pot was brilliant with flames, the one next to it ignited. Little by little, every pot whooshed with fire. With the entire room illuminated, the enormity of it was on full display.

"Wow." Ali pulled herself out of the water and placed the journal in her pocket. "What is this place? It's bigger than a baseball field."

Hundreds of sarcophagi littered the room. Some were in the outlines of people, others just plain rectangles that tapered at the bottom. Like a stretched diamond.

"It's a necropolis," Bait said. "Figaro, trot a bit forward would you?"

Figgy complied, the ever-obedient friend.

A shiver crawled down Ali's spine. "A what? I've heard that word before."

"Look," Bait said. "See that archway in the back? It's the symbol. The gold pyramid with the all-seeing eye above it! It must be Pharaoh Zico-bus's tomb." A wooden door sealed it from the rest of the enormous room.

"Wait," Ali said. "Necropolis? What's that?"

"It's a cemetery of sorts," Bait said. "See all those sarcophagi?"

"The coffins?"

"Yes, well, technically they are sarcophagi," Bait continued. "Each sarcophagus contains a mummy. Some are on platforms, and others are contained within mausoleums, those small buildings on the side there. Come look." He swam a few excited circles in his jar. "They're really quite amazing."

They walked down a broad stairway into the necropolis. Ali slowly approached one. He was right, they were incredible. Running her fingers over the old wood, she traced the outlines of a face. But it wasn't wood. "No, it's clay," she murmured. She assumed it was meant to look like the person when they were among the living.

It also made her sad. The only coffin she'd been around was her mother's. Her heart raced. Even then, she was very young, and her mind had protected her from remembering too much about that day. But now, it was flooding back. Her dad trying not to cry and comforting her, Ali not understanding why her mom wasn't coming back.

"This is incredible," Ali's voice echoed.

"They give me the willies, human," Figgy said. "Can we just see what's behind that archway? You've been standing there for ten minutes."

"I have?" Ali shook her head. "I didn't realize how mesmerized I'd become."

A weird feeling shifted in Ali's stomach.

"These necropolises have many spirits floating around," Chicaletta said. "It is best not to dilly-dally."

"I wouldn't mind a jingle jangle," Tristan said.

They shuffled toward the archway as a group. At first, it appeared the sarcophagi were scattered randomly. But as they walked, it became apparent it was more of a maze. Ali had to concentrate to keep her legs moving forward. Something in that room was nagging at her to linger.

In the far reaches of the room a crash sounded and startled the group. Figgy jumped and tripped over his feet, slamming into the side of a coffin. The whole sarcophagus slid as if it were on ice and bumped into the one next to it. Figgy's hooves clopped on the sandstone floor until he regained his balance.

"Geez," Tristan said. "Are you trying to squish me? Watch where you're putting those big old hooves."

"Sorry." Figgy hung his head.

"It's okay, Figgy." Ali dropped back and gently stroked his soft fur. "That noise scared me too."

Bait tapped the inside of the glass mason jar with his fin. "What's most curious is that the sarcophagus slid with no effort."

Chicaletta pushed on the side on one. It slid as easy as ice. "Things that move, move easily. We should not question the technology of the ancient Egyptians"

"I barely touched it," Figgy said. "I promise."

"Oh, really?" Tristan marched up to the nearest sarcophagus and pressed his small hand against it. "You're saying if I just push a little on one it'll slide across the room."

Tristan pushed, and the thing slid completely

across the room, bumped into another, and caused a chain reaction. The old coffins groaned, and the clay ones cracked.

Everyone turned to Tristan.

"What?" He shrugged his shoulders. "It was an accident."

"One must not disturb the dead unless it is absolutely necessary," Chicaletta scolded.

An almost human groan stole Ali's breath for a moment.

"Stay calm, but we must hurry," Chicaletta said.

No one spoke a word. Each heartbeat pulsed through Ali's ears. They'd disturbed the departed, and Ali knew it. They sprinted to the archway and paused. Only ten stairs separated them from Pharaoh Zicobus's tomb.

Rushing up the stairs, Figgy was the first to skid in his tracks. Ali ran into his rump.

"Sorry, Figgy." She stared at the large stone door.

"Look," Figgy said. "Do you see?"

Ali saw. They all did. In the middle of the tomb door was a wooden square with symbols carved deep into it. It adorned the door like a Christmas wreath.

"Maybe it's just a decoration," Ali said. "Come on."

Stepping around the mini burro, Alison Liv Isner palmed the golden doorknob and pushed.

CHAPTER 14

Nothing.

Locked.

"I don't understand," Glenda said. "We've come all this way. Maybe there's a key under the mat."

"There is no lock." Chicaletta brushed her hand over the cool door. "We are missing something. There are many puzzles in life that we must solve. And it seems like this is one of those."

Ali's hands shook. Mummies. She was surrounded by mummies. *Dead people. A lot of them.*

"We've got to get out of here," Ali said breathlessly. She twisted the doorknob frantically. "We have to do something! Now! Go!" She was on the edge of hysterics. She didn't want to die by a mummy attack.

"Alison." Chicaletta took Ali's head in her hands. She stared deeply into her eyes. Ali felt a sense of calm with that. "One must not underestimate oneself. You are stronger than you think. Do not be afraid."

Ali nodded silently. A thick cord protested in her throat. She swallowed it down hard, ignoring her fear. She pulled Chicaletta closer and embraced her in a hug.

"Thank you, Chicaletta," Ali said.

"Chica," Bait said. "Love, come have a gander. I don't have a great vantage point, but I think there's something to this sign."

"Yes." Chicaletta studied it. After a few moments, a slight tremor rushed through her body. Her hair swished from side to side. "Tristan, the sarcophagus was easy to move, yes?"

"I'm pretty strong," Tristan said. Laying on the ground, he was nearly asleep on the floor. He yawned. "But it wasn't too hard to push. Easy, really."

"It is a puzzle! I may have found a solution," Chicaletta said. "I think this," she said, pointing to the sign, "is a map. It shows the pattern in which we need to arrange the coffins. It is a bird's-eye view, if you will."

"What will moving a bunch of stiffs around do besides make me tired?" Tristan asked.

"I believe it is the key to unlocking the tomb door," Chicaletta said. "Let us get to work. Glenda, you will be paramount in this. Can you fly above us and direct us as to where to move each one according to the guide?"

"Totally," she squeaked.

Walking carefully, they spread out around the room. All but Tristan quickly learned you had to move them with the slightest of touch or they'd slide wildly out of control. Moving them was easy. Glenda was efficient for a bat and had an extremely good memory. She'd fly to the door, come back, and direct all five of them as to where they should move their sarcophagi.

With each move, a small plume of dust would be released when the sarcophagus locked into the right place. Soon the necropolis filled with a hazy dust. It smelled of old, musty bandages, like the antique shop that was next to Ali's father's store.

Tristan pushed one thoughtlessly, and it slammed into another coffin. Everyone's attention was on him. He shrugged. A linen-clad hand burst through the clay sarcophagus. Then the one next to it kicked a leg through the side. Another sat up, and the coffin burst into dust. Mummies moaned to life.

"Hurry!" Ali yelled. "Glenda, how many more do we have to move?"

"Just a few," she said. "Figgy, turn yours perpendicular. Ali, yours needs to rotate ninety degrees. Chicaletta, move it three feet to the left. Tristan, do not touch anything!"

"No problem," he said. "I'm good at doing nothing."

They all did as Glenda instructed.

Grinding stone on stone drowned out the mummy's moans.

"What was that?" Ali asked.

Glenda glided toward Pharaoh Zicobus's tomb door. "It's open! Hurry."

Chicaletta chopped at a limping mummy near her with a machete. The arm fell off and hit the ground in a plume of bone dust. Figgy reared up and kicked the chest of another. It exploded into a pile of brown powder and bandages. Tristan did nothing, as instructed, but then he quickly darted up to the open tomb door and waited.

"Tristan," Glenda said. "Go help! The mummies!"

"What do you want me to do?" He sat. "Make them deader?"

Ali dodged and weaved in between each sarcophagus, careful not to disturb the pattern they created. She ducked under the outstretched arms of a female mummy. Her long, gray hair hung out of the falling cloth wraps around her head.

Ali's heart had never raced faster, and her hands were shaking so hard. Her legs felt like jelly.

She stopped in her tracks. A mummy stood between her and the stairs. Panting, she stared at the door. Everyone had made it but her. She remembered Chicaletta's advice and calmly pulled an arrow out of her quiver and loaded it into the crossbow. After pulling it back, she released it with expert precision; it landed directly in the mummy's stomach. The mummy slumped. Ali jumped over it.

A cold hand wrapped around Ali's ankle. She fell forward, landing on her forearms. Eyes wide, she turned to see the mummy sitting up, holding her foot.

"No!" Ali yelled. She kicked at the mummy and tried to scramble backward toward the stairs. "Help!"

"I'm coming, human!" Figgy trotted off the stairs.

The mini burro fearlessly ran up to the mummy and kicked its arm. It exploded into a plume of dust.

"Come on," Figgy said.

Ali sprang to her feet and stumbled onto the stairs. "Thank you, Figgy. I don't know what I would have done without you."

"Shucks, human, you've helped me this whole way. That's what friends do. Eloise taught us that."

"Mom," Ali whispered.

"It is time," Chicaletta said. She pointed at the door.

Ali placed her hand on the cool golden knob, then twisted it. To her delight, it opened. She ran in and held the door until everyone was in. Figgy backed up to the door and held it closed with his rump. Everyone, even Tristan, was silent as they took in the room.

It was cool and dry. It had ten-foot-high ceilings and was the size of a large bedroom. The musty air smelled of stale herbs and rotting corpses. Light shone up from the centerpiece of the room.

"Pharaoh Zicobus," Ali whispered.

The pharaoh sat mummified in a throne in the center of the room. His arms had been perched on the armrests of the throne. Long spears pierced the back of each hand. From far away, it looked as if he was holding a weapon in each hand. The headdress atop his head was adorned with gold and turquoise stripes running down a broad strip of leather that fell onto his shoulders. On the crest of the headdress was a gold pyramid and the all-seeing eye.

"This entire tomb," Bait said. "It's his sarcophagus, isn't it?"

"Looks that way," Ali said. "Who's going to get the headdress?"

"Not me," Glenda said. "It totally freaks me out."

"You've done enough," Ali said. "You really shined today. You *all* really shined today."

"Yeah," Tristan said. "As long as there are no pretties for the pretty, she's all right."

"Whatever, Tristan," Glenda said. "Since I'm

out, who's going to get it?"

No one volunteered.

Ali sucked in a sharp breath. "One of us will be a grave robber."

She didn't feel good about it, and she was certain her friends didn't either.

Tristan scurried up to the pharaoh and sat in his lap. "Is this guy dead?"

"Tristan, no," Glenda said. "Get down from there."

"Oh, he's not dead?" Tristan smirked and tilted his head up at the mummy. "For Christmas I'd like some pâté and a bicycle. Oh, and a juicy orange." He laughed and laughed.

"Tristan," Glenda gasped. "Stop that."

"Actually," Bait whispered, "this could work to our advantage."

Tristan carried on, listing a number of things he'd like, then burst out laughing like a maniac.

"Tristan," Bait said. "I hate to interrupt, but would you mind unhooking that headdress and bringing it here?"

"Not now." Tristan waved him off. "I'm busy. This is the most fun I've had all day."

"Right," Bait said. "But you know, the Geese could be here any second. So, when you find the time, please bring that here and you can return to . . . whatever it is you're doing."

He ran up behind the pharaoh and unclasped the headdress. It fell into the mummified pharaoh's lap. Tristan tugged the strap and pulled the headdress along the floor toward the group.

"Here." He deposited it at their feet. "Now, I've got a few more things on my wish list I gotta tell ol' stiff."

"Tristan," Glenda scolded. "That is so disrespectful."

"Fine." He shrugged. "But you guys need to lighten up."

"It's wooden and leather." Ali gently picked up the headdress. "I thought these were made of fine silk?"

"Maybe that's what made it special, human," Figgy said.

"Maybe," she murmured.

"Let me have a look," Bait said.

"Here." Ali placed it in front of is jar.

"It's actually olive wood," he said. "It's abundant in the area. But I agree, it's highly unusual for a headdress to be made of *any* wood."

"Now what?" Ali asked.

"Tristan," Glenda said. "Stop that."

"I'm just checking him out," Tristan said. He scurried up one side of the mummy, then down the other. He stood in front of the mummy. "This guy st—"

Poof.

The mummy imploded. Dust filled the room. Ali closed her eyes, covered her mouth with her sleeve, and coughed.

"What did you do?" Glenda squeaked. "I warned you."

"He was already dead." Tristan crossed his arms. "I just made him deader."

As the dust settled, Ali blinked hard a few times. A beam of light shot up from where the pharaoh had been sitting.

"Wait," Figgy said. "I think he may have found us a way out."

"I did?" Tristan asked. "I mean, of course I did. It's always Tristan to the rescue. Tristan, get the headdress. Tristan, tell the pharaoh what you want for Christmas. Tristan, make the pharaoh implode."

"Whatever," Glenda said, brushing past Tristan. "I just want to get out of here, take a bath, and give myself a manicure."

Tristan continued. "Tristan, pretend to be a baby bird. Tristan . . ."

Ali ignored all of this banter and was enchanted with the headdress that she cradled in her palms. She stared at it closely. On the center of every gold stripe was a single gem. She quickly discerned the repeating pattern. Ruby, diamond, emerald, sapphire.

"It's beautiful," she said to herself.

Alison Liv Isner lifted the headdress to her head.

CHAPTER 15

"No!" Bait yelled.

"Huh?" Ali shook her head from side to side. The headdress was inches away from adorning her crown. "Oh, I—I don't know what came over me." She placed it on the ground. "I'm sorry, it felt like I was a million miles away. I don't understand."

"That is why it has been hidden away for all these years." Chicaletta picked it up. "It is a temptress. Now that you know the dangers, you must be strong. Fight off temptations." She tied it on Figgy's back with a coarse, frayed rope.

"Maybe I shouldn't hold it again." Ali said.

"I trust in you," Chicaletta said. "You are clever. You will not make the same mistake twice." She looked to the opening, where the pharaoh had once sat. "There is no time to waste."

"Hey." Glenda fluttered up from the hole. "It's a short drop, then a hallway. I can hear the haboob raging outside. We're close. You guys, I think I hear the drums too. We did it!"

Ali closed her eyes and could almost make out the dull beat.

She ran to the edge and peered down.

"I'm not climbing in there," Tristan said. "This must have been the sewer to Santa's toilet."

"Oh, Tristan," Ali laughed. "You know darn well that was the Pharaoh Zicobus."

"Ready, human?" Figgy asked.

"Ready." Ali took Chicaletta's hand, and they jumped together.

Immediately the cool air turned to hot, dry desert air. Ali landed with a thud. Chicaletta, while strong and agile, landed as light as a feather.

"Look out," Figgy called.

He landed on all fours with an audible "Oof!"

Tristan followed and landed on Figgy's rump. Glenda flew down last.

Ali and Chicaletta took the lead, weapons drawn. The Geese had become an unspoken threat, but there was no need to take chances. Now that they were so close to the outside, they had to be ready. Wind swirled against the tunnel. Ali steadied herself.

With every step the wind howled louder. The stifling heat worsened. Ali's shirt clung to her.

"We're close. I can feel it." Ali kicked at some sand. "The haboob has whipped sand in here."

"Good," Tristan said. "That donkey *stinks*."

"Yes, yes," Bait said. "And you smell like roses, I'm sure."

"Thank you." Tristan puffed his chest out. "I'm glad someone noticed."

"Shh," Ali said. "Do you hear drums now?"

"I do." Figgy sidled up to Ali and nudged her free hand with his head.

She petted him sweetly, his singed hair from the fiery spears tickling her fingers.

"We made it." Ali's heart thumped. But this time it wasn't from fear. It was excitement. "Let's go!"

Ali swung her crossbow on her back and ran. At the exit, she skidded to an abrupt stop. The haboob raged outside. Visibility was zero, and the sun barely shone through. But fifty feet in front of them was a perfectly clear path. It was as if a clear plastic tube had been directly attached to the opening. At the end was the high priest, Chuwen.

This time Chuwen wore what Ali assumed was fit for a pharaoh. A royal blue and white skirt hung lazily to his knees. A thick, gold belt wrapped around his waist, and a jeweled cat face attached to it hung down the front of the skirt. He wore no shirt. Thick, beaded strands of yellow, red, and blue were stacked around his upper arms and around his neck. A matching royal headdress made of fabric rested atop his head, making him appear several inches taller. He looked different than last time, but the drums and the staff confirmed his identity. In his right hand, just like before, was a gnarly, large wooden staff that was taller than him. At the top was a perfectly polished sapphire the size of a grapefruit.

Waving his hand, he beckoned them to come to him. Ali took a tentative step out of the pyramid and into the haboob. Sand swirled all around her, but as she walked to the priest it was calm. Walking up to him, Ali knew what to expect this time.

"Very good." Chuwen's hands were outstretched, and the staff rested in the crook of his arm. Ali untied the headdress from Figgy's back and placed it in his hands. "My child, you have saved the world from catastrophic events through your unwavering motivation to finish a most difficult expedition." He lifted it to his head. Ali gasped. It dissolved when it touched his crown. He lifted his staff toward Ali.

"Wait," Ali gasped. She turned to her friends. "I'll see you soon, I hope." She embraced each one. They all accepted her affection, even Tristan.

"You will, my dear," the priest said. "In due time. You've become quite the adventurer. Adventurous Ali."

The priest tapped Ali on each shoulder, and she blacked out. She awoke on the Persian rug in the storeroom in the back of her father's store.

"Ali," her dad called from the storefront. "Get cleaned up. We're going to the Millers' for dinner."

Ali was out of breath. "Sure, Dad. I'll be right there."

She pulled her mother's journal from her pocket. She opened it to the Egypt Expedition. It read: *Accomplished 10/01/1935.*

Alison Liv Isner had completed her mom's expedition, again.

THE END

Tyler H. Jolley is five foot sixteen inches. By day he is an orthodontist and by night he is a sci-fi/fantasy author. He carries a curse with him each day—too many fun book ideas and too little time to write them. There isn't a place or time that ideas don't slam into the creative squishy part of his brain. Fun facts: he hasn't puked since 1996, he loves pencils, and mountain biking. Writing and riding are a big part of his life.

His debut novel, EXTRACTED came out in 2013 with Spencer Hill Press, and has been a Spencer Hill Press Best Seller, as well as an Amazon Best Seller. PRODIGAL and RIVEN, the second and third books in The Lost Imperials series were released in May of 2015.

THE SOCIAL CAPITAL QUOTIENT

HOW TO RETAIN LEADERS & CULTIVATE YOUR LEADERSHIP LEGACY

Augustine Emuwa

Justine Gonzalez

SCQ Ink

The Social Capital Quotient
How to Retain Leaders & Cultivate Your Leadership Legacy

Published by SCQ Ink

Printed in the United States of America.

ISBN-13: 978-1-7365357-0-7
Library of Congress Control Number: 2021901007

Copy Editor: Kate Shoup
Production Editor: Kate Shoup
Interior Designer: Shawn Morningstar
Interior Layout: Shawn Morningstar
Indexer: Kelly Talbot Editing Services
Proofreader: CDL Editing LLC

DEDICATION

To YOU, the leader who seeks to build a legacy with intentionality and impact far beyond yourself.

May you find the experience of reading this book as cathartic as we did reflecting on and writing it.

Our leadership experiences—both highs and lows— are embedded throughout this book in the honesty and openness of our words. Backed by research and feedback from expert advisers, we offer you this tool to enable you to explore the deeply introspective path that is leadership.

TABLE OF CONTENTS

FOREWORD

BY EDWARD MORRIS, JR.

I am uniquely blessed and honored to have had the opportunity to train many leaders in the education space and other non-for-profit entities. After my time as a principal in Chicago Public Schools, I served as the executive director of instructional leadership across all programs at New Leaders, Inc. (formerly New Leaders for New Schools).

I met Justine and Augustine (a.k.a. Augie) in 2012, during my first year as a regional trainer and coach with the Aspiring Principals Program with New Leaders. That year was an immersive experience for us all, as it focused on providing weekly training and comprehensive coaching support. New Leaders, Inc. had approximately 11 months to prepare Augie, Justine, and other passionate educators across the country to take on the world of educational leadership. During my time at New Leaders, I had the opportunity to influence many other ripe and ready "Justines" and "Augies." I have since moved into another arena of leadership within the national education space and launched my own leadership consulting firm.

You may not be aware of the influence or collective reach of New Leaders in the education space. To date, New Leaders has trained more than 3,200 educators who are leading schools, networks of schools, and districts located across the metropolitan areas of Chicago, Memphis, New York City, Oakland (California), New Orleans, Baltimore, and Washington D.C. During my time as an executive leader with the organization, its reach expanded to other districts in Illinois, Texas, Florida, Georgia, and Michigan. This gave me considerable experience in assessing the impact of leaders and in developing suites of supports and trainings to shift the way leaders influence those in the social sector.

I share this brief summary of my professional experience only to impress upon each reader the "busy-ness" that life brings for leaders like us who are intent on being change agents. I have seen every form of brilliant passion turn into out-of-control zeal, sacrificing effort and time to a misaligned vision. I have had to help leaders become aware of blind spots in their style of engagement because they were not open to becoming deeply connected with the community that existed before they arrived. I posit that there is a deep and critical need for understanding how to gain and maintain social capital to help communities achieve their vision and mission.

The essence of what is articulated in this book challenges readers to move beyond the self. I believe this essence is a consequence of the shared burden of the authors. Since I first encountered Justine and Augie in 2012, I have been impacted, impressed, and intrigued by their maturity and balance as leaders and their willingness to assume the enigmatic roles they have taken on. During my own humble beginnings as their coach, I learned so much from them; I still find it hard to believe that they still consider my voice "ear-worthy."

Over the years of regular check-ins with Augie and Justine, I have had the opportunity to thought-partner with them on educational leadership moves, small business strategies, and real grassroots-driven core principles of how to bring lasting change in other people's lives. With every touchpoint, I carried a strong but quiet sense that these two amazing leaders were tapping into something profound that would have large-scale impact for leaders who are genuinely driven by deeply anchored passion. With every conversation, we have investigated what truly lies beneath the lifecycle—the influencers and the outlying variables of an organization that attempts to serve its mission as one unified body of people. Are they effectively functional or eminently failing because of individual passions and perspectives?

Justine and Augie's work in the field of social enterprise has been deeply participatory. Their successes—and failures—that contributed to this work will create powerful paradigm shifts for leaders looking to harness (not control) the power of influence as participatory and cooperative influencers.

This volume, as the first collective book project by Justine and Augie, brings together a unique spectrum of their life experiences and consultative engagements. They have successfully peeled back several previously hidden layers of what makes for a healthy and sustainable culture in the often disruptive body of social enterprising. Therein lies a very impressive feat. Engaging dense notions of applied sociological concepts, they have compressed and simplified hard work for readers. Justine and Augie gently demand complex cognition through richly scaffolded reading constructs, especially through their smart use of modern parables and case studies. The soul of the individual reader will likewise be inspired with caring intention, especially when using the reflective/self-assessment exercises that book-end each chapter.

Above all, I want to leave you, the reader, with one fundamental promise as you engage these pages: I promise that social impact leaders (principals, center directors, non-profit executives, etc.) will find the Social Capital Quotient framework articulated within this book highly accessible. Readers can easily understand, study, and apply the lofty but achievable notions expressed by these authors primarily because both Augie and Justine have had to live by these principles in varied environments over their time as leaders. That is experience and knowledge that I trust and eagerly entrust to you.

Edward Morris, Jr. is the founder and president of VisionPort, LLC., a leader-centric firm focused on strengthening leadership intelligence through strategy, training, and leadership coaching. Ed also serves as the vice president of programs and services with Branch Alliance for Educator Diversity.

INTRODUCTION

WHAT IS SOCIAL CAPITAL QUOTIENT (SCQ)?

In our 35+ years of combined experience in education and nonprofit sectors, we've seen plenty of examples of organizations that failed to thrive over the long haul. We've also encountered countless leaders who have never considered their leadership legacy. We came to believe that these problems were related—and we wanted to help organizations solve them both.

When we began the process of developing materials to achieve this aim, we wanted to create sustainable solutions. Our research led us again and again to the importance of social capital in organizational longevity and leader legacy. Thus, the Social Capital Quotient (SCQ) framework was born.

There are lots of definitions of social capital. We like the one put forth by Adler and Kwon (2002), which describes social capital as "the goodwill available to individuals or groups," whose source "lies in the structure and content of the actor's social relations" (p. 23). You can think of SCQ, then, as the ability of an individual to harness social capital to build positive relationships. The SCQ framework emphases the use of SCQ to build relationships that promote a positive leadership legacy, which in turn helps foster organizational longevity.

The SCQ framework is based on synergy. It suggests that if individuals in organizations lead with the recognition of others' value or worth—of each person's gifts, talents, and assets—as the primary driver of success, and the organization develops an ecosystem in which individuals help one another improve, then the organization can retain leaders, develop inclusive systems, and thrive at optimal levels. We call this the Theory of Change. (See Figure I.1.)

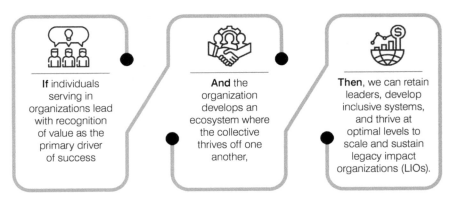

FIGURE I.1: THE SCQ THEORY OF CHANGE.

In developing the SCQ framework, we had to explore what developing social capital *feels* like. We discovered that at its core, social capital feels like all parts of a whole thriving in harmony with each other—a successful ecosystem. The long-term impact of any organization stems from the systems that work collectively together. Achieving this takes deliberate effort.

Is the SCQ framework a magic pill to "cure" ailments like high turnover, lack of employee engagement and investment, non-compliant behaviors, resistance to change, and so on? No. But it can revolutionize leadership practices, further the impact of your personal leadership legacy, and promote organizational longevity. Simply put, a leader's SCQ can affect the viability—indeed the very existence—of an organization.

The Four Elements of SCQ

Both individuals and organizations have measures that comprise their Social Capital Quotient. These measures are based on the four key elements (see Figure I.2):

- **Retention (element 1):** This element relates to who people are and what their value is.

- **Cultural leadership (element 2):** This element pertains to how we view ourselves and the world and how we treat people.

- **Value-driven systems (element 3):** This element has to do with why we operate the way we do and what we believe as a collective.

- **Scalability and optimal functioning (element 4):** This element is about what actions will yield improvements in the short term and long term.

This book focuses on element 1: retention.

Each element contains various indicators intended to drive decision-making, actions, implementation, and accountability. (See Figure I.3.) For example, the indicators for element 1 are as follows:

- Leader morale
- Leader engagement
- Leader retention
- Creating conditions for success
- Planning for succession

 **Retention**
Element 1

 **Cultural Leadership**
Element 2

 **Value-Driven Systems**
Element 3

 **Scalability & Optimal Functioning**
Element 4

FIGURE I.2: THE FOUR ELEMENTS OF THE SCQ FRAMEWORK. (THE RETENTION ELEMENT IS COLORIZED BECAUSE IT'S THE TOPIC OF THIS BOOK.)

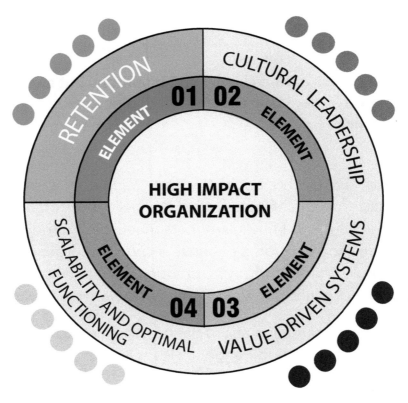

FIGURE I.3: THE SCQ FRAMEWORK.

When properly implemented, each element can positively affect:

- Individual leadership capacity building
- Organizational collective action and efficacy

Each element must be measured and optimized in the right order to ensure success. For example, if a leader were to first focus on element 4, they would find additional barriers that could have been addressed with indicators in element 1. So, if an organization must solve scalability issues by creating and hiring more positions but has no strategy for recruitment and retention, it will create more work, risk, and struggle. Each element is intended to strengthen and enhance the next.

Many organizations have good intentions but end up with larger issues as a result of disconnected indicators.

As mentioned, this book—the first volume in a series—focuses on element 1: retention. We believe an organization's ability to retain quality personnel is a byproduct of the value it places on personnel and on the organization as a whole. Starting with the retention element will set you and your organization up for long-term positive impact.

At its core, retention is about the heartbeat of human relations. It's about being hungry to learn about the potential of another human being. By studying those we serve, we can more easily identify their core attributes and foster the best conditions possible to help them thrive. (This, of course, has the added benefit of delivering better and more sustainable results.) But all this starts within ourselves. We must dig into our own potential before we can dig into anyone else's.

> **The issue of retention is especially critical right now, as workplace culture evolves and norms shift. That's why we focus on retention first—well, that and the fact that retention is what we consider a "right now" issue that can't be ignored!**

HOW TO USE THIS BOOK

There are guidelines that anyone serving in the public service sector can follow to accurately measure and develop their SCQ and, by extension, their viability and the longevity of their organization. As you might have guessed, this book focuses on the guidelines that relate to the retention element.

We started this series with retention because reducing turnover is critical to organizational sustainability and longevity. Incredibly, however, for most organizations, retention (and succession planning, which is closely related to retention) is at best an afterthought. This is a problem. Despite traditions to the contrary, social-serving leaders aren't chained to their current organization. They are free to choose where they want to go!

We believe this book offers solutions to improve retention outcomes for current and future leaders *right now*. In simple terms, this book provides:

- An interactive, personalized, and self-reflective experience
- Multiple tools for evaluating individual and collective indicators within any organization
- Actionable steps for creating value within your organization

The first five chapters in this book focus on the five indicators of the retention element:

- Leader morale
- Leader engagement
- Leader retention
- Creating conditions for success
- Planning for succession

These chapters teach you how to improve your SCQ and strengthen your leadership legacy.

All five of these chapters walk individuals and organizations through a series of interactive and reflective learning protocols. To that end, they contain the following sections:

- **Overview:** In this section, we share a personal anecdote aimed at helping you connect with the theme and focus of the chapter.

- **Why It Matters:** This section brings forth some current and relevant research to show why the indicator within the element of retention is important.

- **Cautionary Case Studies:** Our case studies are based on real-life scenarios we have encountered over the years. Each case study is designed to help you relate what you are learning to real-life scenarios. (Of course, names have been changed in these scenarios.)

- **Questions for Self-Reflection:** Each case study is followed by guiding questions to help you process and synthesize the case study. This also provides you with an exercise rooted in self-discovery, helping you reflect on what you have learned and how you can apply it to yourself.

- **Individual Inventories for Self-Awareness:** Each indicator has its own inventory for your own personal development. Use this inventory to further develop an awareness of self and leadership. Be sure to note your scores.

- **Organizational Inventories for Collective Efficacy:** These organizational inventories should be used within and across teams to evaluate the team's overall perception and where the organization measures in relation to the indicator for the chapter.

A WORD ON CASE STUDIES

Throughout the first five chapters in this book, we discuss outcomes of school leaders' choices in tough situations. We use these leaders—principals, headmasters, or chancellors (*directores de escuela*)—as examples because they are among the most consequential leaders in the world. After all, they're the ones who directly impact the trajectory of our children's lives! These individuals serve as brilliant case studies to illustrate the impact of the social capital quotient on *any* organization, whether it's in the educational sector or a different industry altogether.

The book's final chapter discusses our roadmap tool. This tool is designed to be a GPS of sorts, helping you synthesize your inventory scores, zero in on goals, and create actionable next steps for positively affecting retention while also designing your leadership legacy. This tool can also help you record your thoughts and ideas in an intentional way—something we both wish we'd had in the past! Our hope is that it will serve as a powerful support during your leadership journey by helping you establish milestones for individual and organizational growth.

Just as a GPS might provide different routes to your destination, there are many paths to build your SCQ. No matter what route you take, we assure you, you *will* reach your destination!

CHAPTER 1

LEADER MORALE

*Morale is the fruit that grows
from the roots of communication,
actions, and intentions.*

OVERVIEW

When you take on the title of leader, you have to realize that an important indicator of success is leader morale. Leader morale is a leader's mental and emotional condition—their enthusiasm, confidence, loyalty, and so on—which correlates with their ability to function as individuals, within groups, and among those they lead. Leader morale has a direct effect on leader engagement. It's what enables leaders to engage at their highest capacity in a way that's authentic and meaningful. This improves their ability to be self-aware, which in turn assists in their development as a self-actualized leader.

How can you measure leader morale? The answers to the following questions are good indicators:

- Do you feel the organization supports you and others?
- How does the organization support you and others?
- How do you advocate for support from the organization and others?

None of these questions should be considered in isolation. A holistic interrogation will yield better results.

We often find ourselves partnering with schools and organizations that have communicated that "staff morale is just really low right now." This is often because leader morale is low. If leaders are not valued and supported through organizational actions that improve their morale, it becomes extremely difficult for them to promote staff morale and organizational morale in general. (Think of organizational morale as the way an organization looks, feels, behaves, and performs in its efforts to further its mission while collectively owning and overcoming obstacles that threaten that mission.) Instead, leaders rely on tasks and activities to promote morale. This practice often ignores crucial questions and fails to identify pain points, meaning problems go unaddressed.

> **When morale becomes a task rather than a natural outcome of high leader morale, responsibility for it often trickles down to middle managers and those they lead. The result is almost always a tendency toward mission drift—a clear barrier to long-term success and innovation.**

Unfortunately, when you finally notice that morale is low, it just means that it has gotten bad enough that you can see the overt behaviors that grow from rotten or diseased roots. These roots are communication, actions, and intentions, and they are interwoven into complex layers tied to our personal identities, beliefs, and values. It is no surprise that it often requires anonymous surveys to unveil issues related to morale.

Let's be clear: If you are finding out through a survey about morale issues, it is because you have not established trust and belonging within your organization and/or have not clearly advocated for your needs as a leader. In other words, your own leader morale may be suffering, and the morale of the people you lead might be, too.

Can external factors be related to a period of low morale? Absolutely. Can effective leaders work through these obstacles by acting strategically, listening, and providing adequate support and space for solutions-oriented attacks? Again, absolutely.

> **For leaders to positively affect morale they must first value themselves, so they can see, hear, and value others just as highly.**

In many situations, there is not one specific person or department to "blame" when morale is low. Low morale is the collective outgrowth of weeds and rotten roots that were never properly tended to when they first reared their ugliness. Perhaps they were covered up with soil or rocks (initiatives and programs that distract from the root) or trimmed back temporarily (superficial celebrations that make people feel good for a moment but do not address systemic, broken root systems). But they were never excised completely.

One of our most treasured teachers of leadership, who currently teaches at Georgetown University, consistently challenged us (and still does) to "get on the balcony." In other words, he says, get off the dance floor and head upstairs to get a broader view so you can see what's really going on. This means making it a priority to conduct root cause analysis, gather feedback, and examine all stakeholder perceptions. If you, as a leader, do not create the space to process issues, you may find out about the surprising depths of your morale problems through a survey.

Ineffective communication from both an individual and the organization takes us back to the questions at the beginning of this chapter. We urge you to consider them again and to jot down your responses.

- Do you feel the organization supports you and others?

  _____

  _____

  _____

  _____

- How does the organization support you and others?

  _____

  _____

  _____

  _____

- How do you advocate for support from the organization and others?

  _____

  _____

  _____

  _____

Learn From My Leadership Mistake

Owning Your Personal Contribution to Morale

A while back, I was serving in a regional administrator position at a nonprofit, tasked with coaching high school administrators, developing local boards, and fundraising for 10 high schools, in addition to wearing many other hats. When it came to the organization I worked for, I had drunk the Kool-Aid. Lots of it. The word "adoration" comes to mind in describing how I viewed the organization. Its mission and vision were incredible. And I'd been really successful there. I had launched one campus in a matter of three months of planning and got a promotion within four months of that campus being stable with enrollment, staffing, and funds.

My absolute favorite part of my position was coaching and providing feedback to administrators—in other words, connecting with people. In my role I also worked to develop and streamline systems of accountability where I could share data and feedback transparently while celebrating growth.

One day, I was asked by the organization's founder to "begin building a case" against one of the highest-performing administrators in my region. The founder did not like the tone of some Facebook posts made by the individual—in particular, about the Black Lives Matter movement—and wanted to push the administrator out. Imagine my shock! My morale plummeted.

The truth was, low morale had been a consistent problem within this organization, like it is in many nonprofit and educational organizations. I just didn't see it at first.

Think of morale like a weather forecast. Just as we can make clear predictions based upon current weather conditions, we can predict future problems within an organization based on the current morale. For example, if staff members do not feel supported by their teammates, we might be headed for stormy weather. Worse, we will be totally unprepared when the storm hits. By shedding light on how people feel about the organization, we can brace for bad weather or perhaps even take steps to avoid it altogether.

I made the mistake of ignoring the "weather forecasts" in my organization. I didn't register the low morale until I finally felt it myself, when I realized there were patterns of unethical and discriminatory behavior. I knew that leadership had been unresponsive to deeper retention issues related to morale, but thanks to my ego, I thought I could change things. I had also failed to communicate what boosted my morale—what energized me to continue showing up. Ultimately, I needed to own my contribution to low morale—for my own sake, and everyone else's.

WHY IT MATTERS

As human beings, we want to belong. So, it's no wonder that research shows that people are less likely to leave organizations when they feel they belong.

"I belong" can be expressed in various ways:

- I feel valued.
- I feel supported.
- My voice is heard and valued.
- I am compensated adequately for my worth.
- I am asked about my opinion.
- Those who I report to know pieces of who I am, what is important to me, and what makes me tick.

Morale is most often linked to how supported employees feel.

Of course, this list is not exhaustive. But it provides a good starting point for understanding the path to higher morale within organizations. This list could also help you uncover what is most important for you as a leader.

According to a 2019 article in *Harvard Business Review*:

> *"If workers feel like they belong, companies reap substantial bottom-line benefits. High belonging was linked to a whopping 56% increase in job performance, a 50% drop in turnover risk, and a 75% reduction in sick days. For a 10,000-person company, this would result in annual savings of more than $52M." (Carr, Reece, Kellerman, & Robichaux, 2019.)*

And yet, according to the same article, approximately 40% of people do not feel like they belong at work. In fact, they feel isolated. Imagine for a moment what it might feel like to report to a work setting every day and feel alone. Like you don't fit in. Like no one sees you or hears you. It would be terrible!

Have you ever heard someone described as a "negative Nancy" or "negative Ned"? These terms are used to describe people who are excessively and disagreeably pessimistic. In a work setting, it's often the case that people with this reputation simply feel isolated—like they're not seen or heard.

Having employees who feel this way isn't just bad for those employees. It's bad for the organization as a whole. Indeed, their negative behavior can affect everyone's morale. This is especially true if they possess authority—even if it's just of the informal variety. But if the organization's leadership can find and extract their value, they can become a powerful asset...and our own lives as leaders may also be improved. Perhaps Daniel Goleman, author of *Social Intelligence: The New Science of Human Relationships*, says it best:

> *"...when we focus on others, our world expands. Our own problems drift to the periphery of the mind and so seem smaller, and we increase our capacity for connection —or compassionate action." (Goleman, 2006.)*

If we do not help those we lead feel connected and supported, they will find other ways to be heard and seen. Providing support is not just about making someone feel good, however; it is about taking intentional actions to ensure people are seen and valued, which benefits the organization in the long term.

CAUTIONARY CASE STUDY

Often, leader morale issues are multi-layered, involving competing existential personal questions that we must ask ourselves as leaders. This case study is designed to help you dissect a dilemma with multiple such issues, players, and plays, requiring you to "get on the balcony." Difficult as this may be, it is required work!

Tatiana is a nationally recognized leader in political policy and public administration. About a year ago, she was recruited to work for a national educational nonprofit that has consistently produced high-level leaders in philanthropy, policy, and other public service sectors. Having matriculated through the program herself, Tatiana was thrilled to return to the organization and serve under the current CEO, who was also one of her mentors. She was all in.

During her first year on the job, Tatiana brought together alumni and new funders nationwide to raise more than $1 million in support for the program and negotiated a vital partnership with an Ivy League university. But since then, she has noticed troubling behaviors within the organization. Ultimately, Tatiana has concluded that the organization's board of directors is neglecting its fiduciary responsibilities. Many of the funders with whom Tatiana has forged important relationships have come to believe the same thing.

Tatiana has begun asking questions but has received no satisfying answers. In an attempt to quiet Tatiana, the chairman of the board has offered her a compensation package in return for her resignation—in other words, a bribe. Tatiana feels as if all her hard work is undervalued. She feels isolated, under-supported, and even abused.

Tatiana is caught in a dilemma. Should she do the ethical thing and confront the board for its malfeasance? Or should she remain loyal to the board, stay quiet, and step down?

To consider what Tatiana should do, answer these questions:

- What is at stake for Tatiana if she does not resign?

  _____

  _____

  _____

  _____

- If you were Tatiana's personal mentor (outside of the organization), how might you coach her?

  _____

  _____

  _____

  _____

- Who is to blame in this situation?

  _____

  _____

  _____

  _____

QUESTIONS FOR SELF-REFLECTION

Now that you've had time to reflect on another person's dilemma, look inward and reflect on where you are with leader morale.

- With whose thoughts and opinions am I most concerned when I make decisions? For example, am I most concerned about the thoughts and opinions of stakeholders or some other group?

  _____

  _____

  _____

- True or false: Systems and structures are mainly driven by the needs of those I lead. Why or why not?

  _____

  _____

  _____

- Do you believe there is value in leaders being celebrated? How often are you celebrated?

  _____

  _____

  _____

INDIVIDUAL INVENTORY FOR SELF-AWARENESS

Score how you perceive current leadership practices, attitudes, behaviors, and actions with respect to leader morale. (You'll refer to the total score in Chapter 6, "Designing Your Leadership Legacy.")

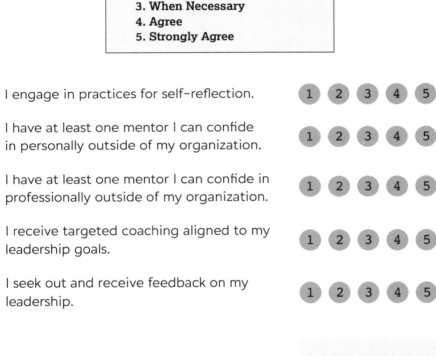

KEY

1. Strongly Disagree
2. Disagree
3. When Necessary
4. Agree
5. Strongly Agree

I engage in practices for self-reflection.　　1　2　3　4　5

I have at least one mentor I can confide in personally outside of my organization.　　1　2　3　4　5

I have at least one mentor I can confide in professionally outside of my organization.　　1　2　3　4　5

I receive targeted coaching aligned to my leadership goals.　　1　2　3　4　5

I seek out and receive feedback on my leadership.　　1　2　3　4　5

My Total for Leader Morale: _____

ORGANIZATIONAL INVENTORY FOR COLLECTIVE EFFICACY

Describe how your collective organization perceives current leadership practices, attitudes, behaviors, and actions with respect to leader morale. (Again, you'll refer to the total score in Chapter 6.)

```
                    KEY
        1. Strongly Disagree
        2. Disagree
        3. When Necessary
        4. Agree
        5. Strongly Agree
```

Our organization values self-reflection.　　① ② ③ ④ ⑤

Any current or aspiring leader in our
organization has access to mentorship.　　① ② ③ ④ ⑤

Team members' personal goals are very
important to those to whom we directly　　① ② ③ ④ ⑤
report.

Team members' professional goals are very
important to those to whom we report.　　① ② ③ ④ ⑤

Anyone in our organization can seek out
coaching.　　① ② ③ ④ ⑤

My Organization's Total for Leader Morale: _____

ADDITIONAL THOUGHTS

Use this space to jot down any additional thoughts you have about leader morale.

_____

_____

_____

_____

_____

_____

_____

_____

_____

_____

_____

_____

_____

_____

_____

_____

_____

_____

CHAPTER 2

LEADER ENGAGEMENT

*It is in the best interest of your
organization to consistently
reflect and ask if there's still
passion within the team
for what you are doing.*

Overview

What do leaders and kindergarteners have in common? To explain the indicator of leader engagement, we looked to the inception of much of our human socialization and engagement: kindergarten.

Pasi Sahlberg is an esteemed visiting professor at Harvard Graduate School of Education who previously served in the Finnish Ministry of Education and Culture. In his recent book, *Finnish Lessons 2.0*, Sahlberg outlines expectations for teaching kindergarten pupils. (Stay with us here because what we found is fascinating!)

In his book, Sahlberg posits that kindergarten teachers are responsible for just three things: "enhancing the personal well-being of children; enforcing behaviors and habits that take into account other people; and increasing individual autonomy gradually." (Sahlberg, p. 52.) He continues, "Kindergarten in Finland doesn't focus on preparing children for school academically. Instead, the main goal is to make sure that all children are happy and responsible individuals."

To us as professionals, this may sound like a lot of fluff—like the school system in Finland is about hugs, rainbows, and cupcakes. However, Finland has the highest performing schools in the entire world. Consistently. As in, for decades.

So, what can we learn from this and apply to our own leadership journeys and to the ongoing growth of the organizations we serve? Simply put, it's that the fluff—the touchy-feely stuff—matters.

Having productive conversations with leaders in your organization around their beliefs and values—in other words,
fluffy conversations—will determine the long-term success
and performance of your organization. This involves more
than a one-off chat, however. In other words, holding one
barbecue around a campfire will not convince people to
magically open up! Rather, you need to work over the long
haul to establish a connection with your organization's
leaders—to gain access to them in a way that enables you
to better guide them and help them evolve in a manner
that is mutually beneficial.

When we consider our engagement with leaders, we must
begin by asking what we expect from them, and if our
expectations are aligned with the expectations of those
they lead. In other words, much like kindergarten teachers,
we must focus on the overall goals—in our case, of the
organization.

Remember: Finland's students don't perform well because
of high-stakes tests, schedules, or mandates. They perform
well because they:

- Take ownership in the learning process
- Operate within a stimulating environment that has been
  created intentionally and is focused on facilitating
  their growth

The same goes for leaders. Like Finnish students, leaders
associate care with the perception that someone is personally invested in their well-being. In the context of a
professional environment, this means leaders feel set up
for success because the things they strive to achieve are

noticed, applauded, and linked to larger organizational goals and values. As teams demonstrate connections rooted in deep understanding—a form of relational and social capital—the natural byproduct is inherent motivation.

THE IMPORTANCE OF PERSONAL CONNECTION

Justine here. When I began my journey in school leadership, one of my coaches advised me not to smile until halfway through the school year. This coach really believed that a school leader should put on a serious front to students, parents, and the teaching staff. Needless to say, I could not be without my smile. So, I ignored my coach's advice. In doing so, I quickly realized that the more honest and transparent I was with my team of teachers—in other words, the more I was "myself," smiles and all—the more willing they were to trust me. And the more I allowed them to feel comfortable sharing—again, by being my authentic, smiling self—the more we could band together as a team to serve students. The bottom line: There is something special about deeply knowing who you are serving alongside!

THE IMPACT OF CARE AND COMPASSION

We see demonstrating care and compassion—for yourself and those you lead—as involving something bigger than just feelings and emotions. It's a mechanism that can be mindfully used as leverage to scale specific positive practices throughout an organization. The idea is that if everyone is seen and developed with care and compassion, their productivity should increase thanks to their personal investment and a deep desire to contribute in an exceptional way—kind of like the kids in Finland's schools.

If you find that this is not happening, the question becomes, how does one lead people in a way that garners the best possible results? Answering this question will require introspection and deep reflection. This calls for an environment that supports self-discovery and the identification of strengths and areas of potential growth.

To quote Albert Einstein, "Once we accept our limits, we go beyond them." But we must begin with ourselves as leaders. If we cannot name, accept, and reflect upon our actions and behaviors, then we cannot change for the better. Once we accept where we are in our journey, we can go beyond the limit that may not have even been determined by the organization we serve but rather by our own mindset. This brings us back yet again to kindergarten in Finland. As simplistic as it seems, most of us have worked or currently serve within organizations where:

- We are unsure of what is expected of us as leaders.
- We don't know how organizational goals are linked to the people we lead.

It's important to be intentional as you examine how you engage in the following practices:

- Self-reflection
- Evaluating ongoing goals for your personal and professional life
- Staying connected to others within and outside of your current role

Just as leaders—no matter their title—need coaching and mentorship, they also greatly benefit from collegial networks that challenge them both intellectually and philosophically. We can't always control the nature of the organizations where we lead, but we can control how our professional experiences take shape—and by extension, how engaged we are.

NAVIGATING THROUGH TURBULENCE

When we fly in airplanes, the pilot always tells us that in the event of an emergency, our first duty is to move quickly to don an oxygen mask. The same is true when leading others. That is, only when your own oxygen mask is on can you do your best for your team and ultimately your organization.

When you know what you need, you place yourself in an offensive position—better able to advocate for yourself based on what supports are available. Ongoing introspection helps you engage on a more authentic level and "manage up" no matter what comes your way. Just because the organization where you lead might be experiencing turbulence doesn't mean you have to!

WHY IT MATTERS

Engaging with the self means knowing ourselves intimately enough to be confident in critical engagement with employers from the very beginning—that is, when they extend an offer for employment. We've heard of principals being hired because of their LatinX background and new executive directors being brought on due to their track record with moving data metrics.

These types of superficial criteria for hire are simply not enough and may point to hasty decision-making ulti- mately not working in your favor. It is vital to have a deeper conversation with executive teams looking for candidates. Ideally, these qualities should directly tie into the orga- nization's mission, vision, and core values. This is because these act as anchors to dictate what people do and why they do it. (Obviously, for this to happen, the organization needs to have clearly articulated its vision, mission, and core values in the first place!)

Once leaders accept employment, it's easy to lose sight of what matters most: setting their team(s) up for success. The consistent hum of "productivity" often results in unin- tentional silos that create barriers between colleagues and departments. Instead of focusing on care, we become task-driven. Moreover, those in leadership roles often find it difficult to engage with those they lead without mak- ing it all about the work. "What will my employees think?" they wonder. "How do I maintain professionalism while also being authentic?" Let's be honest: It's much easier to com- municate policies and new products or initiatives to those you lead than it is to communicate values, beliefs, and emotions!

In the nonprofit and educational sectors, we see consistent concerning parallels that relate to how leaders are engaged and how they engage themselves. As we wrote this book, we asked leaders questions like, "What are you reading?"

Or even more basic questions like, "How are you?" We found that many of them were so inundated with tasks that they had lost sight of much of their personal identity. This meant they were unable to "show up" authentically for their staff—often with devastating effects on their teams' ability to move forward.

As leaders, we often think our work is about schedules, processes, and policies. But in fact, these are driven by how effectively a leader is able to reflect, learn, grow, and apply new skills.

THE IMITATION GAME

Albert Bandura's *Social Learning Theory* proposes that we can acquire new behaviors when we observe and imitate that of others (Bandura, 1976). Ask yourself, who are you imitating and why? Losing sight of our own identity limits our chances to "show up" for others and these behaviors trickle down as norms of "doing business" in our organizations. When we know this to be true, we more consistently make the time to reflect on our practices and behaviors as leaders. In turn, we acknowledge our role in getting what we need, and use this to champion the things that we know to be important. This is deeply vital for organizations that are evolving their practices to support leaders.

Leaders who stay fixed on technical and task-oriented actions are called *passive leaders*. In contrast, *active leaders* focus on the value of the self and others to deliberately operationalize tasks for the greater good. All leaders should consider where they fall in terms of active versus passive leadership. One easy way to do this is to examine how you use your time and language when communicating with others. (See Figure 2.1.)

How Passively Engaged Leaders Spend Time	How Actively Engaged Leaders Spend Time
Completing compliance reports and paperwork	Connecting with people
Developing lists so items can be checked off	Determining daily priorities that have the most impact on strategic goals
Relying on systems that are focused on making their role easier	Relying on systems that are focused on creating better results for the people they serve

Passively Engaged Leaders May Say Things Like	Actively Engaged Leaders May Say Things Like
"I won't be able to make that meeting because I leave at 3 p.m. every day."	"Can we find a time to connect that works for all of us?"
"Just call my assistant to make an appointment with me. I don't have time to manage my calendar."	"You can contact me directly via [preferred form of communication]."
"I'm not really sure who created that policy. I'm just doing my job."	"Maybe we could brainstorm some ways to make sure our policies are relevant. Who else should offer input?"

FIGURE 2.1: ACTIVE VERSUS PASSIVE LEADERS.

Learning Moment:
Why Should I Swim with Dolphins?

In Warren Berger's 2014 text, *A More Beautiful Question: The Power of Inquiry to Spark Breakthrough Ideas*, he tells the story of a former executive at the tech company, Oracle.

"...Marc Benioff, an executive at the tech company Oracle who took an extended break from his job so he could just think. Benioff journeyed to India and then continued on to Hawaii, where, as he told the authors of *The Innovator's DNA*, he went swimming with dolphins in the Pacific Ocean. Out there in the water, he thought of a question: "I asked myself, "Why aren't all enterprise software applications built like Amazon and eBay?" This inspired Benioff to launch Salesforce.com, which set out to use the Internet to radically change the design and distribution of business software programs. Within eight years, Benioff's company had $1 billion in sales and was credited with "turning the software industry on its head," (Berger, p. 77). If we examine Benioff's scenario, he was not seemingly disgruntled with his position or pay at Oracle. In fact, it sounds as though he was valued so much, he could take a leave of absence to swim with dolphins. This is a powerful picture because he started by engaging himself.

Cautionary Case Study

Leader engagement can look very different depending on the clarity (or lack thereof) within an organization. Still, leaders must develop an awareness of how the legacy they are building factors into their personal development and extended opportunities. At the end of the day, regardless of the dynamics at play within an organization, it's our job and our responsibility to determine how our engagement can be mutually beneficial to us and those we serve. This case study offers you a chance to critique the character presented with regard to his leadership challenge.

After serving a local school district for nearly 20 years, Shaun—a first-generation college graduate who "made it out" of the marginalized neighborhood where he grew up—was thrilled when he was asked to serve at a low-performing school in this exact same community. After all, Shaun was one of the only people around who could understand the unique character and challenges of the area.

Shaun has served as principal of this school for almost three years now. He has consistently seen an increase in student performance. Shaun has also replaced some teachers who have left to ensure that he has the best team possible. He prides himself on the systems and processes he's implemented, including maximizing his master schedule to provide common planning times for every teacher.

Although Shaun has led the school's turnaround, there hasn't been additional support or funding to help the school move forward. When he meets with his superintendent for his annual evaluation, he expresses frustration over this fact. In response, Shaun's superintendent questions his loyalty to the school.

For three years, Shaun has consistently put in 15-hour days. He has devoted so much time to fixing a school that has been marginalized for decades that he hasn't stepped back to consider his next move or what will happen if his contract is not renewed. He thought he could trust his superintendent, but now he feels as though he can't even confide in her about the future.

- What is at stake for Shaun?

_____

_____

_____

_____

- Is Shaun an active or passive leader? How do you know? (Refer to the "Why It Matters" section for a review of these terms.)

  _____

  _____

  _____

  _____

- How might Shaun have engaged himself?

  _____

  _____

  _____

  _____

- If Shaun is ready to resign tomorrow, and you were called in to coach him, what introspective process would you want him to go through?

  _____

  _____

  _____

  _____

QUESTIONS FOR SELF-REFLECTION

Now that you've had time to reflect on another person's dilemma, look inward and reflect on where you are with leader engagement.

- How engaged are you as a leader? Rate yourself from 1 to 5, with 1 being "not at all engaged" and 5 being "extremely engaged." How do you know?

  _____

  _____

  _____

  _____

- What practices do you use to engage with yourself and how do you measure self-improvement?

  _____

  _____

  _____

  _____

- What would you need from your direct supervisor to help facilitate deeper reflection and introspection?

  _____

  _____

  _____

  _____

- Would you consider yourself an active or passive leader? Why?

  _____

  _____

  _____

  _____

INDIVIDUAL INVENTORY FOR SELF-AWARENESS

Describe ways in which you increase your level of engagement. (You'll refer to the total score in Chapter 6, "Designing Your Leadership Legacy.")

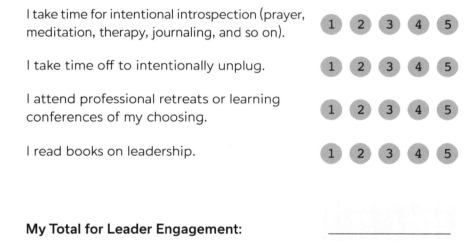

KEY

1. Strongly Disagree
2. Disagree
3. When Necessary
4. Agree
5. Strongly Agree

I take time for intentional introspection (prayer, meditation, therapy, journaling, and so on). ① ② ③ ④ ⑤

I take time off to intentionally unplug. ① ② ③ ④ ⑤

I attend professional retreats or learning conferences of my choosing. ① ② ③ ④ ⑤

I read books on leadership. ① ② ③ ④ ⑤

My Total for Leader Engagement: _____

Organizational Inventory for Collective Efficacy

Describe current practices implemented within your organization for engaging current and aspiring leaders. (Again, you'll refer to the total score in Chapter 6.)

> ## KEY
>
> 1. Strongly Disagree
> 2. Disagree
> 3. When Necessary
> 4. Agree
> 5. Strongly Agree

Mindfulness and other strategies for introspection are encouraged in our organization.

① ② ③ ④ ⑤

The mission, vision, and core values of my organization reflect a clear commitment to my growth and development.

① ② ③ ④ ⑤

Our leaders live and embody our mission, vision, and core values.

① ② ③ ④ ⑤

Attending professional retreats or learning conferences of our choice is encouraged.

① ② ③ ④ ⑤

Our organization is a professional learning community that believes in assuming positive intentions, engaging in inclusive and equitable decision-making, and courageously tackling difficult conversations because we know they help us grow.

① ② ③ ④ ⑤

My Organization's Total for Leader Engagement: _____

ADDITIONAL THOUGHTS

Use this space to jot down any additional thoughts you have about leader engagement.

_____

_____

_____

_____

_____

_____

_____

_____

_____

_____

_____

_____

_____

_____

_____

_____

_____

_____

_____

_____

CHAPTER 3

LEADER RETENTION

*Become very clear on who you are,
what you are able to do, and how that
complements the organization
you are leading.*

OVERVIEW

Retention tends to be dealt with through a reactive lens. That is, it's an afterthought rather than *the* thought.

Unfortunately, when we think about retention after someone leaves, we perpetuate the cycle of hasty hiring that tends to not only hinder progress toward goals, but also disrupt agreements within teams. This is a problem because it takes time for people to buy into these goals and agreements.

Curriculum experts Jay McTighe and Grant Wiggins famously made backward-design the hallmark of teacher lesson planning. But although education professionals across the nation have been trained in this practice, few take the same approach when it comes to retaining employees—especially leaders.

Our difficulties with retaining leaders have a detrimental effect on social capital—the ability for one to function effectively within a team in a way that supports the whole. When leaders in key management and supervisory roles transition without transparent and inclusive planning, we often see drops in team morale and production, which hinders progress for everyone.

The impact of a leader staying with an organization or leaving a legacy behind can each be critical to the long-term trajectory of that organization.

A mutual connection of ours in the greater Chicago area is currently the CEO of a large organization, where he leads 100+ individuals. Now in his seventh year, he leads an organization that, at the start of his tenure, struggled to produce consistent results for both staff and stakeholders.

When he was recruited for the position, he sought professional coaching on how he should apply for the role. This enabled him to become very clear on precisely what skills and experiences he brought to the table and how these complemented the organization he was seeking to lead. By the time he secured the position, he had galvanized many leaders and stakeholders to support his role. He tapped this group for coaching when determining who else to bring onto his team.

This leader secured what we call *advisory autonomy*. In other words, he had coaches and advisors who oversaw his actions but gave him room to blossom.

We've boiled down advisory autonomy to three core ideas:

- Transparency and trust
- Authentic goals that connect with strategic support
- Strengths and growth areas internalized by all parties

This leader now models the same process with every person he hires, emphasizing relationships, connection, and collaboration. This enables him to actively maintain his position, produce consistent results, further his areas of expertise, and create an environment for distributive leadership.

This person has had numerous leadership opportunities with multiple national and local organizations—opportunities that have enabled him to continue to build his personal and professional network. However, he remains in his role because he has made the choice to remain at this same organization.

This is a story of retention that is often not told—a story we all wish we could live ourselves. But perhaps we *can* live out this story if we understand the mirror-effect of value—knowing our own value and seeing this reflected in those we lead.

WHY IT MATTERS

If you are familiar with the work of Patrick Lencioni—books like *The Advantage* and The *Five Dysfunctions of a Team*—then you've probably heard that trust is the foundational driver for results. The ability of an organization to build trust directly correlates to its ability to retain top-level leaders.

Part of building trust is understanding the value of each individual on our team. When we understand the value of each individual, we can lead them—and ourselves—more effectively. Showing genuine curiosity about the hopes and dreams of those we lead models care and compassion and ignites collaboration. You must also understand your own hopes and dreams. In our experience, a good way to do this is to develop a personal vision statement.

Building trust is just one way to influence retention. Another way involves a bit more creativity: cage-busting. Of course, all these efforts involve investment in some form or another. The following sections discuss developing a personal vision statement, cage-busting, and investing in retention in more detail.

Developing a Personal Vision Statement

Having a personal vision statement can have a significant impact on how we make decisions on a daily basis. It also reveals what we value about ourselves, which influences what we value about those we lead. Incredibly, most high-level leaders we know do not have a personal vision statement—but they should!

Here is a good example of a personal vision statement:

> *Luke helps others gain financial freedom and strives to end the poverty cycle in marginalized communities.*

When composing your personal vision statement, keep these points in mind:

- Your vision statement should be one sentence.
- Your vision statement should involve a couple of key action words.
- Your visions statement should be conceptually broad but encompass your passions.

Composing your personal vision statement involves identifying your passions, desires, and gifts. To identify these, start by answering these questions:

- What gets you excited to hop out of bed each morning? (PASSIONS)

_____

_____

_____

_____

- What are the problems you'd like to help solve in our world? (DESIRES)

_____

_____

_____

_____

- What are your top three talents? (GIFTS)

_____

_____

_____

_____

When composing your personal vision statement, you might also want to consider your life's work. This is because your personal vision statement will become a baseline to determine which opportunities you respond to with a "yes" and which ones require a "no."

Finally, ask yourself, if you were to leave your role tomorrow, what would you want others to say about you? Your answer to this question should help guide you in identifying your personal vision statement. For more on developing a personal vision statement, see Chapter 6, "Designing Your Leadership Legacy."

"A Man Is a Sentence"

We aren't the first people to suggest the development of a personal vision statement. It's said that an advisor to President John F. Kennedy suggested that he (Kennedy) develop one. The story goes that when Kennedy first became president, he was a bit all over the place. This advisor urged Kennedy to embrace the idea that "a man is a sentence"—in other words, people should seek to sum up their legacy in one concise and compelling sentence.

Cage-Busting

Frederick Hess introduced the idea of *cage-busting leadership* as an avenue of innovation for educational leaders. His 2013 book, *Cage-Busting Leadership*, describes how so-called "cage-busters" can find ways to get creative about opportunities:

"Cage-busters find ways to create new, hybrid roles that permit good educators to take on new responsibilities, assist more kids, or impact students more deeply—and to be recognized or rewarded accordingly." (Hess, p. 44.)

By way of example, Hess recounts a story of a school principal who persuaded teachers to take on extra duties for no pay by rewarding them with assistance qualifying for a local leadership development program, ultimately observing that "People are often more motivated by opportunity, recognition, or excitement than a couple of bucks." (Hess, p. 44.)

Could a strategy like this be applied to better equip an internal pipeline of leaders? What if this became a core avenue for retaining leaders within an organization? On a related note, how often do you just promote someone internally who may not necessarily have the capacity because...well...it's just easier than hiring someone new?

Ultimately, it comes down to value. What we value is where we focus our energy, efforts, and leadership. Our idea of what brings value to the overall organization is directly reflected by what we most value within our own role.

INVESTING IN THE FUTURE

Allocating funding to develop leaders can be a struggle—particularly for educational organizations and nonprofits. To address this, we suggest you consider the long-term return on investment of developing your current leaders. This development might involve sending someone to a conference, hiring an executive coach for a few of your leaders for six months, or organizing a leadership retreat for those you believe are most committed to the future of the organization.

Identifying the ROI

In a 2019 article on Forbes.com, contributor Chris Westfall posits that organizations spend an estimated $166 billion each year on leadership development in the United States alone. Yet, most of this training doesn't work—at least not in terms of retention. Many industries continue to experience abrupt transition among valuable members.

On a related note, research shows that there isn't enough attention placed on the development of soft skills and organizational culture. With the steep price tag associated with developing leadership, organizations—especially those with scarce resources—must spend wisely. This means they need clarity on what the right ROI is for them.

Efforts that facilitate the retention of strong leaders result in consistency and legacy-oriented workflows, which in turn drives results. So, if you're looking for an ROI that includes sustainable results, you must be prepared to evaluate your beliefs about what you deem essential learning when you invest in leaders.

You should also make mindful decisions on who you invest in. Sometimes we determine which employees attend events or conferences or receive opportunities based on their title or on the number of years they've been with the organization. Instead, it's usually better to make these selections based on people's goals and potential.

Here are some questions you might ask when considering whether to invest in a particular employee:

- Do they want to grow within the organization?
- Do you know their personal and professional goals?
- How have they demonstrated mastery in their current role?

If you are selecting people for whom you cannot answer these questions, you might reconsider who you are investing in and why you have deemed them valuable.

CAUTIONARY CASE STUDY

In this case study, we see how mid-level leadership roles can often be overlooked. This could be due to a lack of value on the part of the individual and communicated by the organization either directly or indirectly.

Victor is the program coordinator for a mid-sized non-profit that serves multiple states in one geographic region. Due to employee-retention issues, Victor is considered a veteran, despite having served in his role for only two and a half years. Although Victor has heard the executive leadership discuss the issue of retention, he has noticed that no solutions seem to be forthcoming.

During his time with the organization, Victor has served three different executive directors, and multiple coordinator roles have been created and removed from the org chart.

Victor would love the opportunity to move into a director role and grow his leadership capacity, but if he's really honest, he's been scouring the internet for new roles elsewhere; he has serious reservations about continuing with an organization that seems to turn over its employees like pancakes on a griddle.

Complicating matters, Victor feels a sense of loyalty to the founder of the nonprofit. Previously, the founder was one of Victor's mentors, and actually knows Victor's family. Many times, Victor has been called upon to complete tasks that, quite frankly, a program coordinator should not be doing. The last thing Victor wants to do is let down his mentor, but he also knows he should be honest about his desire to grow in his leadership.

Victor is torn. Should he just go elsewhere, where his desire to grow will be seen? Or should he wait patiently at his current organization in the hopes that someone will recognize what he does and what kind of impact he could have if he were recognized as more than a program coordinator? To consider what Victor should do, answer these questions:

- How does Victor value his role?

_____

_____

_____

_____

- How does the organization value Victor's role?

  _____

  _____

  _____

  _____

- What's at stake for Victor if he leaves?

  _____

  _____

  _____

  _____

- Should the founder take responsibility for low employee retention?

  _____

  _____

  _____

  _____

QUESTIONS FOR SELF-REFLECTION

Now that you've had time to reflect on another person's dilemma, look inward and reflect on where you are with leader retention.

- Who are you most connected to in your current role? Why?

_____

_____

_____

_____

- How do you know you are valued in your current role?

_____

_____

_____

_____

- When people don't feel valued in your organization, who's to blame?

_____

_____

_____

INDIVIDUAL INVENTORY FOR SELF-AWARENESS

Describe your actions aligned to knowing, developing, and providing growth opportunities for leaders. (You'll refer to the total score in Chapter 6.)

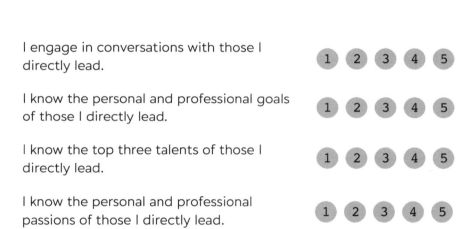

KEY

1. Strongly Disagree
2. Disagree
3. When Necessary
4. Agree
5. Strongly Agree

I engage in conversations with those I directly lead.

1 2 3 4 5

I know the personal and professional goals of those I directly lead.

1 2 3 4 5

I know the top three talents of those I directly lead.

1 2 3 4 5

I know the personal and professional passions of those I directly lead.

1 2 3 4 5

My Total for Leader Retention: _____

ORGANIZATIONAL INVENTORY FOR COLLECTIVE EFFICACY

Describe your organization's actions aligned to knowing, developing, and providing growth opportunities for leaders. (Again, you'll refer to the total score in Chapter 6.)

KEY

1. Strongly Disagree
2. Disagree
3. When Necessary
4. Agree
5. Strongly Agree

We collaborate with colleagues in our own department/division.

① ② ③ ④ ⑤

We collaborate with colleagues outside our own departments/division.

① ② ③ ④ ⑤

Our organization has a defined path for the pursuit of leadership roles.

① ② ③ ④ ⑤

Current leadership team members value their own development and share learning transparently.

① ② ③ ④ ⑤

My Organizations' Total for Leader Retention: _____

ADDITIONAL THOUGHTS

Use this space to jot down any additional thoughts you have about leader retention.

_____

_____

_____

_____

_____

_____

_____

_____

_____

_____

_____

_____

_____

_____

_____

_____

_____

_____

CHAPTER 4

CREATING CONDITIONS FOR SUCCESSION

To unlock the truth about our own leadership capacity, we must first accept that we will never be the standard of perfection.

OVERVIEW

Turnover in the public service field directly affects the lives of countless people—children, members of certain ethnic and racial groups, people in certain socio-economic classes, and so on. And yet, turnover is often the elephant in the room. People don't like to deal with it head on—usually because doing so might unmask cultural issues that must be owned and accepted.

Transitions that come out of the blue can have damaging effects on an organization's reputation. Undoing this damage can be difficult. Indeed, we've seen examples of schools and nonprofits that have worked for years or even decades to change negative perceptions about them! But the truth is, when team members transition or turn over, it's only a crisis if we don't see it coming and fail to prepare. In fact, staffing transitions can be a great way to generate innovation and opportunity! That's why it's critical to plan ahead—a process that involves creating conditions for succession.

In a perfect world, companies continuously evolve, with staff transition becoming a critical indicator of how effectively social capital creates growth opportunities for leaders.

Creating conditions for succession involves methodically integrating human resource activities to scale the capacity of people within organizations. This in turn fosters leadership outgrowth that allows an organization to continue evolving. Put another way, creating conditions for succession involves working your way out of a job and helping to prepare the next leader in line to take it over!

Unfortunately, we tend to hire in the hopes that people will stay for as long as we need them. This mindset inevitably results in disappointment. In an ever-changing society in which roles and responsibilities can change at the drop of a hat, we need to shift to ensuring that our systems recognize individuals for their unique gifts and develop differentiated training and development programs accordingly.

We believe that the way an organization responds to staff transition is a clear indicator of how effectively and proactively it engages with its leaders—current and future. The question becomes, how do we create conditions for succession that are advantageous for both the organization and the individual in today's climate of high turnover? That's the subject of this chapter.

As you read through this chapter, think about the conditions for your succession in your current role and how you might provide the necessary conditions for those you lead.

WHY IT MATTERS

Remember the children's book *Oh, the Places You'll Go!* by Dr. Seuss? It's one of our favorites. We particularly like this passage:

> *You have brains in your head.*
> *You have feet in your shoes.*
> *You can steer yourself any direction you choose.*
> *You're on your own.*
> *And you know what you know.*
> *And YOU are the guy who'll decide where to go.*

Over the years, we've found ourselves regularly referring back to this quirky passage. To us, it means that it's up to us—and only us—to decide how to live our lives. This takes self-awareness and courage. It also means that we have all the tools within us to steer our own course.

Our direction in life is something we own and accept. Instead of solely relying on an organization to build your capacity, it's up to you to understand yourself in a deep way so you can identify what you're capable of and advocate for yourself.

Back in Chapter 3, "Leader Retention," we discussed a leader we know who had been recruited to lead a large organization. We observed that this leader became "very clear on precisely what skills and experiences he brought to the table and how these complemented the organization he was seeking to lead." We bring this up here because it was careful introspection (self-awareness) that enabled this.

His self-assessment was what drove not just his ability to land the job, but to perform it expertly, right out of the gate. More importantly, he was the one who played the most active role in making that determination.

What does Dr. Seuss's classic poem have to do with succession? Simple. We spend our entire lives tapping into our self-awareness and using our tools to move from one phase to the next—to "all the places we'll go." So, from the beginning of each new phase, and maybe even before, we need to plan for the next one—including who will succeed us.

LEARN FROM MY LEADERSHIP MISTAKE:

ASSESSING YOURSELF

Augie here. It was day 1 in my introduction to school leadership under the careful watch of my aspiring principal coaches at New Leaders Inc., a school leadership development institute founded on the campus of Harvard University. I was young and eager, with the will and intelligence to compete among other colleagues interested in school-turnaround work.

I was quickly inundated with critical feedback and professional-development advice I didn't want to face at times. As much as I knew about creating strategic plans, aligning curriculum, and making data-driven decisions, I faltered when it came to introspection.

During my time with New Leaders Inc., which lasted for almost two years, I learned the term *performance orientation*. It describes people who feel the need to showcase their performance rather than their vulnerabilities. But it wasn't until years later, after I'd become a leader myself, that I finally grasped the term's importance.

Simply put, when you're a leader, people don't care what you know, until they know that you care. So, it's critical that you as a leader learn to care for yourself and for others, to do so deeply, and to leverage the resulting relational capital you earn to lift everyone up.

Given my youthful missteps in this area, I frequently ask myself these questions:

- As a leader, how am I demonstrating vulnerability?
- What other ways am I garnering trust from those who I lead?
- What would make my practice in this area even better?

PERCEPTION MEETS REALITY

How we communicate our self-assuredness is how we're perceived by those we lead. Although skillful writing in emails and other technical means of communication is great, it's the *other* cues—things like body language, active listening, and authenticity—that give insight into who we are as individuals and caregivers. We bring this up because, well, perception is reality. So, you must take care not to behave such that people misinterpret you and perceive you to be unauthentic and uncaring.

> People in supervisory roles can send strong messages about their attitudes and feelings about their constituents without saying a word. Like author and leadership expert John C. Maxwell says, "People may hear your words, but they feel your attitude."

Knowing how you come across—and fixing any behaviors that send the wrong message—is critical to creating conditions for succession. Understanding how your leadership feels to others can also provide tremendous insights. These include:

- Insights into talent and untapped potential among those you lead to help identify future leaders

- Insights into root causes of barriers to success

- Insights into how best to delegate responsibilities

All these improve your ability to ensure your successor will be the best possible replacement.

LEADING WITH INTROSPECTION

We leverage trust with our colleagues for a reason: to lead. And as we've discussed, building trust requires knowledge of ourselves as well as of those we lead.

In a professional context, when I know myself and those I serve, I am better equipped to determine who goes where, how quickly or slowly, and how timing might affect their ability to be successful. All this relates to successful successions.

We gain even more trust by achieving our goals—especially when they are challenging. And as we bring our identities to the work, we enjoy seeing how the fruits of our labor fit inside the proverbial fruit basket.

This book discusses several leaders who moved beyond the metrics, exceeding goals that were set for them. These leaders have also evolved to set new goals for themselves and their teams—a reflection of the autonomy they've earned over time. To achieve this, each of these leaders started with introspection and operated from a place of vulnerability.

NAVIGATING YOUR ECOSYSTEM

The snapping dragon turtle is an unlikely leader. A prehistoric reptile that weighs 220 pounds (despite its relatively short length of 26 inches), this animal—which can live to be 100 years old—is slow and usually goes unnoticed. But it possesses certain biological traits and abilities that put it at the top of the chain in bio zones across the country. Snapping dragon turtles positively thrive in their own ecosystems!

Typically, when we envision human leaders, we focus on the mavericks: the high performers who act and look the part. The "snapping dragon turtles"—people who might not look or act like traditional leaders—often go unnoticed. But the mere existence of actual snapping dragon turtles calls into question the efficacy of using traditional criteria to evaluate potential leaders.

When determining who should ascend to higher roles—in other words, when considering who will succeed us—we need to move beyond these traditional criteria. This means re-evaluating systems of inclusion to ensure that mavericks *and* snapping dragon turtles get a seat at the table.

Essentially, what we're describing is an *ecosystem mentality*. In an ecosystem, all parts thrive. The self-actualized leader in an ecosystem sees the value in others and is in the optimal position to put this knowledge to work—including for the purposes of succession planning.

Here are some questions to help you consider the state of your own ecosystem:

- What does your ecosystem look like?

  _____

  _____

  _____

  _____

- Who is in your ecosystem?

  _____

  _____

  _____

  _____

- How did they gain access?

  _____

  _____

  _____

  _____

AVOIDING DISENGAGED LEADERS

Too often, leaders become disengaged. They display a lack of investment in their organization's mission. When this happens we often point the finger at the leader alone. We rarely ask how the conditions within the organization influenced the leader's feelings and actions.

Ultimately, it's the responsibility of both the leader *and* the organization to determine whether the leader is the right fit for the role and how things play out. So, the organization, as a whole, must develop the necessary conditions to engage its leaders.

As part of this effort, organizations must prioritize creating conditions for succession. This might include the following:

- Tapping executive supervisors to directly support and coach at the individual level

- Giving leaders the opportunity to grow their area(s) of specialty

- Replicating positive succession practices across the organization

- Ensuring that diversity both throughout the organization and among leadership feels natural and not forced

SUCCESSION PLANNING: MOVING FROM AFTERTHOUGHT TO CONSTANT ACTION

Earlier we mentioned that from the beginning of each phase, we need to plan for the next one—including who will succeed us. But in truth, we really need to begin planning even before that. This helps explain why many organizations provide incoming staff and even potential employees with personality assessments to measure a variety of aptitudes and psychological characteristics. Mid-level leaders use these assessments to gain an understanding of how people work best based on their self-identified skill sets. They also use these assessments to ensure teams include people with a variety of skills and competencies. This practice helps create conditions for succession.

Aptitude and social character trait batteries are so prevalent because they can really get the conversation started about a person's natural aptitudes and their professional development.

Creating conditions for succession also means:

- Putting in place adaptive systems of support for existing employees who transition into new roles

- Ensuring new hires and existing employees feel comfortable in every part of your organization—and asking ourselves why if they don't

- Encouraging individuals within the organization to consistently assess themselves based on their individual results

Organizations must create and cultivate environments in which leaders are validated, are acknowledged as skilled practitioners, and quickly experience trust from day 1.

As organizations shift succession planning from an after-thought to a mindful practice that occurs before and during a new hire's employment, they tend to create equitable governance practices at the executive level that place value on the experiences of individual leaders from start to finish. Executives prioritize relationships with *all* their leaders at each level to scale human capital across the board.

When this happens, leaders on the front lines support, hire, and transition people through a more legacy-oriented lens. These leaders ask questions like:

- What's the vision for candidates as they enter and leave?

- How is this vision explicitly and transparently communicated?

On the flip side, front-line leaders must embrace professional reflection. They are just as accountable for advocating for experiences and opportunities to further develop their areas of expertise. This is especially true if the organizations in which they work fail to create conditions for succession. It's up to them to reflect on their work and refine practices accordingly.

All this requires us to place value on developing an intimate understanding of ourselves and of individuals we promote or hire to facilitate workloads tailored to their ability and expertise. This moves us away from frenzied or idealistic staffing to establishing and measuring organizational goals based on the leaders we choose to sit in the seat.

The question we constantly come back to is, how are we setting our leaders up for succession? Perhaps more importantly, how are we *not*?

RELIABLE RUBRICS

While researching for this book, we reviewed a variety of leadership rating policies and rubrics used by nonprofits and school districts across the country. We found that many of these are not as comprehensive as they might aim to be. In fact, over the last few years, we've seen a trend of rubrics becoming more and more dense despite the clear existence of correlations between organizational outcomes and work performance evaluations.

We recognize that every organization has a system of governance. So, in our view, "scoring points" means working alongside leaders to identify expectations that factor into performance reviews. Again, trust is increasingly important, so all parties feel comfortable coming together as practitioners with similar goals and interests in mind—in other words, they can nurture the self while upholding the mission.

Simply put, being crystal clear and openly communicating how strengths are viewed and articulated in performance reviews will be paramount if we want to move the needle on multiple performance indicators within our organizations.

CAUTIONARY CASE STUDY

Many of us map our leadership journeys based on passions that stem from our identity and cultural foundations. So, when presented with opportunities that feel like "the perfect fit," we often neglect to set healthy boundaries, romanticize outcomes, and ultimately burn out—hardly creating conditions for succession. This case study depicts such a scenario.

When her local school board tapped Principal Lopez to lead a school in her old neighborhood she jumped at the chance—even though the school, Cesar Chavez Elementary, had seen better days. From the late 1970s through the mid-1990s, Cesar Chavez Elementary had thrived as the premier magnet academy in the neighborhood. But over time, things began to change. The school's rating fell from "proficient with distinction" in reading and math to "partially proficient" in mathematics and "substantially below proficient" in reading. Between 1996 and 2018, the school lost well over half of its average yearly student enrollment. Decisions made by the district, neighborhood divestment, and tensions with political organizations likely all played a part in the school's—and the surrounding neighborhood's—decline.

Upon signing her first four-year contract, Principal Lopez knew the road ahead wouldn't be easy. Indeed, it would be replete with barriers. Despite these hurdles, Principal Lopez was hopeful and inspired—even when colleagues in other parts of the city questioned her decision to take the job.

Her goal was to record significant improvements and restore the school's magnet status, and as a committed leader, she worked tirelessly and fearlessly toward these marks.

Thanks to the addition of programs and resources, and to parental support during the first two years of her tenure, Principal Lopez was well on her way to achieving her goals. But things got derailed during her third year on the job. Principal Lopez found herself working with a new supervisor—her fourth—without the guidance of a mentor. A series of widely publicized incidents of employee misconduct occurred. Student enrollment declined. And budget cuts forced her to eliminate three key positions at the school—one being a key member of her leadership team.

At the end of year 3, Principal Lopez considered resigning from her position as principal, but ultimately remained in her role for the remainder of her contract. She did, however, initiate a search for a new position outside the school district. Meanwhile, the school's rating fell to "substantially below proficient" in both math and reading, student discipline issues peaked, and staff morale plummeted.

- How does Principal Lopez's succession experience measure up?

_____

_____

_____

_____

- Who's at fault? Why?

  _____

  _____

  _____

  _____

- What conditions could have been created to support different results?

  _____

  _____

  _____

  _____

QUESTIONS FOR SELF-REFLECTION

Now that you've had time to reflect on another person's dilemma, look inward and reflect on where you are with creating conditions for succession.

- What conditions for succession have you created for your own succession as well as the succession of those you lead?

  _____

  _____

  _____

  _____

- Describe the support you have in building your own succession plan.

  _____

  _____

  _____

  _____

INDIVIDUAL INVENTORY FOR SELF-AWARENESS

Describe your current conditions and readiness for implementing a succession plan. (You'll refer to the total score in Chapter 6, "Designing Your Leadership Legacy.")

KEY

1. Strongly Disagree
2. Disagree
3. When Necessary
4. Agree
5. Strongly Agree

I have developed a niche of expertise unique to my skill set.

(1) (2) (3) (4) (5)

I have worked to develop my own personal vision.

(1) (2) (3) (4) (5)

I have engaged in strategic opportunities to further develop my professional capacity.

(1) (2) (3) (4) (5)

I have identified the employment opportunities that best complement my skill set(s).

(1) (2) (3) (4) (5)

I have created my own ecosystem of support and know why select people have access to my ecosystem.

(1) (2) (3) (4) (5)

My Total for Creating Conditions for Succession: _____

ORGANIZATIONAL INVENTORY FOR COLLECTIVE EFFICACY

Describe your organization's current conditions and readiness for implementing a succession plan. (Again, you'll refer to the total score in Chapter 6.)

> **KEY**
> 1. Strongly Disagree
> 2. Disagree
> 3. When Necessary
> 4. Agree
> 5. Strongly Agree

Our organization provides opportunities for leaders to showcase their unique expertise internally and externally.

① ② ③ ④ ⑤

We use our understanding of each leader's attributes to continuously adapt as an organization.

① ② ③ ④ ⑤

We actively position leaders to maximize their strengths.

① ② ③ ④ ⑤

Our leaders routinely assess the strengths of those they supervise.

① ② ③ ④ ⑤

When transitions occur, our organization is equipped and ready to support these changes with confidence.

① ② ③ ④ ⑤

My Organization's Total for Creating Conditions for Succession: _____

ADDITIONAL THOUGHTS

Use this space to jot down any additional thoughts you have about creating conditions for succession.

_____

_____

_____

_____

_____

_____

_____

_____

_____

_____

_____

_____

_____

_____

_____

_____

_____

_____

_____

CHAPTER 5

PLANNING FOR SUCCESSION

*If there's one thing I regret about
my own succession, it's that in
the nine years I spent leading, I could
have dedicated more time to intentional
self-work, especially at the onset.*

OVERVIEW

We have both learned quite a lot from our work in and departure from public service. Transitioning from being a school leader to a full-time business owner required shifting skill sets—a task that felt both new and challenging.

If there's one thing I (Augie) regret about my own succession, it's that during the nine years I spent leading, I should have dedicated more time to intentional self-work, especially at the onset. This could have improved my own personal growth in my first year as a leader...and my succession path.

A succession path, especially for those in mid-level leadership positions, should serve as a sort of backward map. It "starts" with the legacy that the leader wants to leave behind and works backward from there. Charting this map involves succession planning—a process that requires considerable personal insight and the desire to leave a lasting legacy.

Presidential Seal of Approval

This brings to mind a recent conversation we had with a business consultant. He mentioned a relative of his who had worked with the President of the United States as a member of his cabinet. He went on to say that on their first day at work, before being assigned any other task, the president gave each member of the cabinet a beautiful, personalized ink pen and a blank sheet of white copy paper. They were then instructed to write a detailed letter of resignation. Naturally, everyone was quite puzzled.

It was quickly explained to them that this task would enable them to identify and understand two key things:

- Their personal and professional goals
- A vision for their legacy

The cabinet members also collaborated to create an inclusive blueprint to guide outcomes for each member and, by extension, the nation.

Talk about planning for succession from day 1! On their very first day at work together, these cabinet members prioritized reflecting and taking ownership. Writing their resignation letter gave them an opportunity to visualize what the end of their tenure might look like. This would enable them to lead from a proactive rather than reactive position.

This story is so important because it provides an example of personnel-centric decision-making. But it's just one example of supporting the internalization of systems designed to build upon legacy. Imagine if that had been your experience. How would it have affected your trajectory?

We share this story because we find it fascinating that despite having collectively served 35+ years in the education and nonprofit sectors, neither of us were ever asked to dig deep within ourselves to align our personal values and skill sets with scalable outcomes that create pathways for those we lead and those who lead us.

The fact is that few (if any) public-school systems or non-profits require new hires to sit down with their supervisor on their first day to talk about their eventual resignation —which, of course, relates to the issue of succession. We suppose that doing so would be seen as taboo. But the story of these cabinet members suggests that maybe it shouldn't be. After all, members of the cabinet of the President of the United States serve at the highest level of government and make decisions that affect millions of lives, and this is how *they* ensure that their goals and the goals of the organization they lead are aligned. Wouldn't it make sense if other leaders—including leaders in educational and nonprofit fields—did, too?

THE PLEASURE PRINCIPLE

How often have we as leaders continued to "push hard for the vision" when we are no longer passionate about it? On a related note, how often do we continue to work for an organization when we no longer find pleasure there? Our experience and research tell us that the answer is, well, pretty often.

We cannot be our best selves or do our best work in these circumstances. This is a problem. Especially for those of us who work in public service, it is *extremely* important that we bring our best selves to work every day. It is our duty and responsibility to do so. This will have a direct effect on the outcomes experienced by human beings with whom we interact and their communities.

Research shows that a lack of pleasure can also have a negative effect on our ability to become self-actualized—which, as you've learned, is a big problem if you're in a leadership role.

Finally, there is substantial evidence that points to a correlation between retention and work satisfaction (i.e., pleasure).

We must consistently think of ways to serve our people better. This is especially true for leaders!

Unpacking Your Leadership Legacy

As you are reading this book, you're probably starting to think about what you want your leadership legacy to be. After all, your leadership legacy has a lot to do with succession planning. Well, now's the time to really unpack that.

Figure 5.1 contains a handy worksheet. Use it to write down your answers to the questions on page 77.

If this is your first time doing this, take a deep breath, and remember: This is your moment!

IDENTITY	AWARENESS

LEGACY
(Remember, make it one sentence!)

GUIDING PERSONAL BELIEFS	GUIDING PROFESSIONAL BELIEFS

FIGURE 5.1: SCQ IN ACTION: BECOMING A SELF-ACTUALIZED LEADER.

- **What are the top four things you want anyone you encounter to know about your identity?** Write down your answer in the Identity section of the worksheet.

- **What are your guiding personal beliefs?** Write down your answer in the Guiding Personal Beliefs section.

- **What are your guiding professional beliefs?** Write down your answer in the Guiding Professional Beliefs section.

- **What are the three talents you use the most?** Write down your answer in the Awareness section.

- **What is one talent you do not have?** Write down your answer in the Awareness section.

- **What is your legacy?** Synthesize your leadership legacy into one sentence and write it down in the Legacy section.

These questions are designed to equip you with deeper insight into how your personal values, identity, and beliefs connect with your vision. Answering these questions is the first step of proactive, or offensive, leadership. It enables you to advocate for learning and enrichment opportunities that grow you and, by extension, your organization.

WHY IT MATTERS

We believe that people who choose careers in public service are called to do so because they are deeply invested in the people they serve. Simply put, practitioners in the education and nonprofit sectors are compelled to make a career out of heart-oriented work.

It's no surprise that so many of us enter these fields with passion and purpose. But few of us actively map our exit route—nor are we coached to do so. Doing so is critical, however—especially if you do it in a way that uses your legacy as your primary GPS.

Recently, we spoke with the executive director of a non-profit whose mission is to end hunger in her region by developing innovative economic and green infrastructure. During our talk, she made this observation:

> *"As an executive director, this is the most challenging yet rewarding position in the world. But I've been told that if I leave, the place may fall apart."*

What does this statement tell you about this leader? What does it tell you about her organization?

Placing Our Finger on the Pulse

School leadership is not for the faint at heart. Sure, we would like it if all school leaders possessed staying power, but this is not the case! Recent studies in education show that (Jensen, 2014):

- Between 20,000 and 25,000 school principals (one-quarter of all principals in the U.S.) leave their posts each year.

- Fifty percent of new principals quit during their third year in the role.

- Those who remain in the role of principal frequently do not stay at high poverty schools.

Further, only minimal disparities exist among races and genders.

Our research and experience reveal that that the flight of mid-level leaders from highly complex institutions can result in devastating consequences for all parties involved. This is true in both the business and public service sectors.

On the flip side, when employees feel like they belong, turnover risk drops by 50% and sick day usage decreases by 75% (Carr, Reece, Kellerman, & Robichaux, 2019).

We think that employees feel like they belong when they believe that they're valued, and that their organization has actively mobilized them to use their talents in intentional ways. This is why, as tough as it is, succession planning—including creating conditions for succession—can no longer be something we do as an afterthought. We must be more deliberate. Remember, like we said in Chapter 4, "Creating Conditions for Succession," the transition or turnover of team members can be a great way to generate innovation and opportunity. It's only a crisis if we don't see it coming and fail to prepare for it!

CAUTIONARY CASE STUDY

This case study tells a story about a leader with innovation, passion, and drive who created an organization to support at-risk youth. Now that the organization has grown, however, she faces complex challenges that she never anticipated. Take a moment to read about her dilemma and compare your leadership trajectory with hers.

Rosie started her career in education as a post-secondary advisor in one of Ohio's toughest high schools. During this experience, she found that nearly half the students she helped shepherd off to college failed to persevere past their sophomore year. Given her deep connection with these students, she began to invite them back for informal interviews to better understand the barriers they faced.

Rosie found that 80% of her advisees left college due to such reasons as financial difficulties, unfamiliar coursework, and so on. But underneath these issues was the reality that the curriculum they completed in high school did not teach them how to be resourceful, solve problems, and advocate for themselves effectively.

Rosie decided to develop an advisory curriculum to better prepare her students for college. Rosie then realized she needed to think bigger. In 2011, she launched CollegePlus, a nonprofit organization whose mission was to prepare students to overcome the challenges of college life.

CollegePlus was an immediate success. Within three years, thefounding members, led by Rosie, raised more than $5 million for college persistence programming and schol-arships. The organization's offerings became highly sought after by high schools serving students below the poverty line.

In 2016, despite its major success, CollegePlus fell under scrutiny for lacking diversity within the staff. In addition, other nonprofit organizations in the education space began challenging Rosie's ability to authentically connect with the community she served, given their difference in ethnic backgrounds.

Two years later, Rosie announced she was stepping back from leading day-to-day operations to focus on fundraising. Many speculated that this decision was encouraged by board members, who believed that hiring a new face for the organization would redeem its reputation and ensure consistent student membership and donor interest.

- What's Rosie's dilemma?

  _____

  _____

  _____

  _____

- What adjustments could Rosie have made along the way?

  _____

  _____

  _____

  _____

- What does Rosie's decision tell you about her?

  _____

  _____

  _____

  _____

- Between Rosie and her board, who's most accountable in this scenario? Why?

_____

_____

_____

_____

QUESTIONS FOR SELF-REFLECTION

Now that you've had time to reflect on another person's dilemma, look inward and reflect on where you are with planning for succession.

- Do you have a professional timeline? If so, how comfortable do you feel sharing this timeline with supervisors and colleagues?

_____

_____

_____

_____

- How would you describe your transition into your current role?

_____

_____

_____

_____

- How will the transition into your role be for your successor?

_____

_____

_____

_____

- If you leave your role, who or what will be affected most? How will this align with larger priorities for the organization?

_____

_____

_____

_____

- If you leave your role, how will you advocate to make it a smooth transition and meet your desired outcome?

_____

_____

_____

_____

INDIVIDUAL INVENTORY FOR SELF-AWARENESS

Assess your individual readiness for succession planning. (You'll refer to the total score in Chapter 6, "Designing Your Leadership Legacy.")

KEY

1. Strongly Disagree
2. Disagree
3. When Necessary
4. Agree
5. Strongly Agree

I know how to identify potential leaders willing to share in leadership responsibilities.

① ② ③ ④ ⑤

I am ready to take steps to intentionally build the capacity of those I lead.

① ② ③ ④ ⑤

I give others the opportunity to shadow me for a day.

① ② ③ ④ ⑤

I have found pleasure in my role.

① ② ③ ④ ⑤

I am confident in the value I bring to my current role.

① ② ③ ④ ⑤

My Total for Succession Planning: _____

ORGANIZATIONAL INVENTORY FOR COLLECTIVE EFFICACY

Assess organizational readiness for succession planning. (Again, you'll refer to the total score in Chapter 6.)

KEY

1. **Strongly Disagree**
2. **Disagree**
3. **When Necessary**
4. **Agree**
5. **Strongly Agree**

Our human resources department offers a defined leader–development program.
① ② ③ ④ ⑤

All team members are encouraged to participate in inventories such as those offered by Gallup, Myers–Briggs, Enneagram, etc.
① ② ③ ④ ⑤

Our organization always seeks to attract and engage new talent, regardless of need (i.e., even without open positions).
① ② ③ ④ ⑤

Our organization prioritizes the individual value that each role contributes to the greater mission of the organization.
① ② ③ ④ ⑤

Organization Average for Succession Planning: _____

ADDITIONAL THOUGHTS

Use this space to jot down any additional thoughts you have about planning for succession.

_____

_____

_____

_____

_____

_____

_____

_____

_____

_____

_____

_____

_____

_____

_____

_____

_____

_____

_____

CHAPTER **6**

DESIGNING YOUR LEADERSHIP LEGACY

*Before jumping to the next steps,
stay in the moment. Settle your mind
on what you are seeing about yourself
and your organization.*

OVERVIEW

This chapter provides you with a roadmap to help you synthesize your inventory totals, home in on goals, and create actionable next steps to positively affect retention while designing your leadership legacy. We hope that this chapter will serve as a guide for active introspection that you will return to throughout your leadership journey. By the end of this chapter, you will have embarked on a course to develop a vision that reflects your skill set and abilities and leads you toward a legacy that you choose and are passionate about.

Before we proceed, let's check your temperature to measure where you are in the current moment. This will enable you to get clear on your vision for your legacy. Answer the following questions...and be honest!

- If you had the opportunity to leave your current organization, would you? Why?

  _____

  _____

  _____

  _____

- How much time have you invested in getting clear on your legacy for leadership? (Circle one.)

  a. I haven't started.

  b. I have begun to think it through.

  c. I am in the process of creating my vision for my legacy.

  d. I've developed ideas that I have shared with at least one person.

  e. I've created and am actively testing my vision in the field.

- How do you know you are moving/leading in the right direction?

  _____

  _____

  _____

  _____

Consider how you answered these questions as you proceed.

Let's also take a moment to review the SCQ framework, shown in Figure 6.1. If you're experiencing *déjà vu*, it's because you saw this figure way back in this book's introduction. We want to show it to you again to remind you that the steps in the framework are never-ending. We draw inspiration from this quote from Nelson Mandela:

After climbing a great hill, one only finds that there are many more hills to climb.

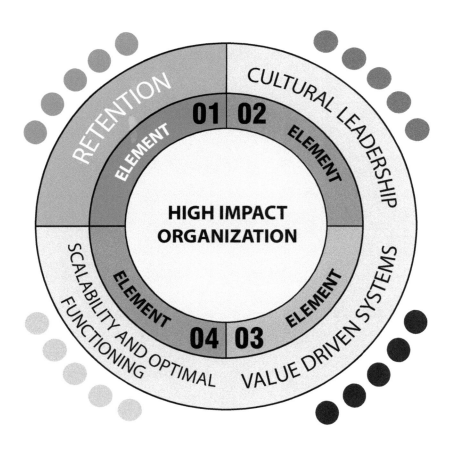

FIGURE 6.1: THE FOUR ELEMENTS OF THE SCQ FRAMEWORK.

REVIEWING YOUR INVENTORIES

We know. The questions in our individual and organizational inventories weren't always easy or fun to answer. But by answering them honestly you can gain critical insights.

These inventories were designed to enable you to assess yourself and evaluate your organization. They're meant to reveal:

- How you see yourself

- How you see and lead others

- How your organization sees and leads you

These revelations are crucial in helping you develop your leadership legacy and thereby improve retention.

So, let's get to it. Go back to the individual and organizational inventories in Chapters 1 through 5 and write down the totals from each one in the following tables. Note which scores are higher (indicating an area of strength) or lower (indicating an area of growth).

Don't think of your totals as "good" or "bad." Instead, think of them as data that you can use to examine your thoughts, feelings, and skills.

Individual Inventories for Self-Awareness (Element 1: Retention)	
INDICATOR	SCORE
Leader Morale (Chapter 1)	
Leader Engagement (Chapter 2)	
Leader Retention (Chapter 3)	
Creating Conditions for Succession (Chapter 4)	
Planning for Succession (Chapter 5)	
TOTAL INDIVIDUAL SCORE FOR RETENTION	

Organizational Inventories for Collective Efficacy (Element 1: Retention)	
INDICATOR	SCORE
Leader Morale (Chapter 1)	
Leader Engagement (Chapter 2)	
Leader Retention (Chapter 3)	
Creating Conditions for Succession (Chapter 4)	
Planning for Succession (Chapter 5)	
TOTAL ORGANIZATIONAL SCORE FOR RETENTION	

After you write down your totals, take a moment to reflect on them. Ruminate on what the indicators are telling you. Here are a few questions to get you thinking:

- What do you notice about your individual inventory for self-awareness?

_____

_____

_____

_____

- What inferences can you make about your organization's collective efficacy?

_____

_____

_____

_____

- What conclusions can you draw given the outcomes of these inventories?

_____

_____

_____

_____

DEFINING YOUR VISION

Now that you have compiled your total scores and pro-cessed your findings, it's time to take action. Figure 6.2 contains a graphic organizer called the "SCQ Leaders Compass." You use this graphic organizer to write down areas of strength and opportunity for you and your orga-nization. You also use it to brainstorm actions you can take for succession planning, individual and organizational leg-acy mapping, and being proactive. Basically, it gives you space to unpack your thoughts and ideas in a meaningful way to better understand actions you might take to design, redesign, or upgrade your personal vision. You can also use it if you engage a trusted advisor to help you develop a plan. The organizer also facilitates a deeper dive into the intersections that exist between your organization's strengths and opportunities for growth and your own.

Remember: Introspective conversations are great. But if you do nothing with the ideas you generate, you're back where you started.

Here are some tips to help you along:

- Start with the easiest parts first—the shaded areas.

- Carefully review the title prompts in the corner boxes. This is where the real magic happens!

- Refer to earlier chapters for examples of specific actions you can take.

- Look for areas of intersection—for example, action items that appear in both individual and organizational boxes. These might be worth prioritizing.

The graphic organizer is meant to support you in identifying the transformational work you want to do in your career as a leader. This type of work is very challenging, but it can be done—*if* you understand and accept who you are and what you need.

Now, let's get started!

If space becomes an issue, visit our website at https://scquotient.com/downloads for an expanded version of this graphic organizer.

SUCCESSION PLANNING	STRENGTHS: ORGANIZATION	LEGACY MAPPING (INDIVIDUAL)
Brainstorm ways to transfer your skill set to others by leveraging the support of a supervisor	Identify elements that are areas of strength	Brainstorm ways to expand your skill set while leveraging the support of a supervisor
STRENGTHS: SELF Identify elements that are areas of strength	**SCQ LEADERS COMPASS** Use this chart to begin identifying your next course of action	**OPPORTUNITIES: SELF** Identify elements that need improvement
LEGACY MAPPING (ORGANIZATIONAL) Brainstorm ways to expand your skill set while leveraging your strengths for organizational impact	OPPORTUNITIES: ORGANIZATION Identify elements that need improvement	BEING PROACTIVE Brainstorm ways to grow your skill set while advocating for yourself with a direct supervisor

FIGURE 6.2: THE SCQ LEADERS COMPASS GRAPHIC ORGANIZER.

ALIGNING YOUR LEGACY WITH YOUR FAITH

One thing we've learned working with organizations in the K–12 public education sector and the nonprofit world is that many people in these fields have a strong connection to their faith, be it Christian, Jewish, Muslim, Buddhist, or what have you. If you are one of these people, you might want to incorporate the tenets of your faith into your vision and legacy—especially as they relate to your relationships with others.

Author and civil rights leader Howard Thurman devoted much of his work to examining the role of Jesus Christ as a teacher and leader. In his text *Jesus and the Disinherited*, Thurman writes:

> Sincerity in human relations is equal to, and the same as, sincerity to God. If we accept this explanation as a clue to Jesus' meaning, we come upon the stark fact that the insistence of Jesus upon genuineness is absolute; man's relation to man and man's relation to God are one relation.

For us, this quote speaks to the issues of leadership and retention because both hinge on human relations. Incorporating your faith in your vision and legacy can help you maintain this focus.

WRITING YOUR OWN CAUTIONARY TALE

American novelist and activist Norman Mailer once said, "Every moment of one's existence one is growing into more or retreating into less." Mailer's quote reminds us that if we fail to evolve, we will not be able to ignite change or develop and live out our leadership legacies.

Failing to evolve is one pitfall. Another is burnout. *Burn-out* describes a state of emotional, physical, and mental exhaustion caused by excessive and prolonged stress. Trust us: "the burn" is real, and it can be incredibly painful! Then there's the risk of becoming numb in your role. Simply put, this won't work. Living out your legacy requires your full presence and attention!

We bring these up to help you see that one aspect of designing your legacy is identifying things that might stand in your way—in other words, to write your own cautionary tale. When you know what to avoid, your path to success will suddenly become clearer! Follow these steps:

1. Turn back to Chapter 5, "Planning for Succession," and find Figure 5.1.

2. In this space, write down the sentence you entered in the figure's "Legacy" area. This is so you can continue to validate it.

_____

_____

_____

_____

- Refer to your entries in the graphic organizer in Figure 6.2 and write down what actions you need to take to design your legacy.

    _____

    _____

    _____

    _____

- Write down any barriers you think might prevent you from taking these actions.

    _____

    _____

    _____

    _____

- Ask yourself, what can you do to avoid these barriers? Use this space to write your answer.

    _____

    _____

    _____

    _____

- Identify the immediate next steps that are essential for your progress and write them here.

  _____

  _____

  _____

  _____

- Write down any advice you would give yourself to stay the course.

  _____

  _____

  _____

  _____

That's it! You've done the work. We hope you have a better sense of your vision and legacy—and how to achieve them both.

PRACTICE COMPASSION

As you undergo this process, we ask you to:

- Be compassionate toward yourself.
- Be compassionate toward others.

We are human beings. We aren't human doings. Don't make this experience all about metrics. Make it about people. Trust us, data-driven results are on the horizon!

A SNEAK PEEK AT ELEMENT 2: CULTURAL LEADERSHIP

At this moment, we each find ourselves with flourishing consulting companies that allow us to walk alongside organizations and their leaders to develop more inclusive environments—especially for people of color. We collaborate to generate data-driven reporting and to create programs that help all kinds of organizations approach anti-racism, cultural transformation, diversity, equity, and inclusion. We've also developed tools to help school administrators and teachers understand the cultural narratives of students and to view their learning experiences through a lens of empathy. It's amazing and transformational work.

This work has been an effective testing ground for a better understanding of element 2 of the SCQ framework: cultural leadership. The topic of the next book in the *SCQ Framework* series, cultural leadership, pertains to the relationship between a person's values, language, and beliefs.

Leaders who are culturally empathetic understand how to navigate situations that they might not have experienced themselves. This requires constant practice, self-regulation, and humility. It also requires a willingness to notice things outside of your own purview.

As leaders, our personal norms, practices, and experiences sometimes prevent us from naturally making objective decisions. Many of the issues that relate to race, equity, and inclusion in the workplace stem from this! Mastering this element of the SCQ framework will give you the tools you need to address these serious and systemic problems.

Final Thoughts

Thank you for working with us to define your legacy and improve retention. We hope it's been both powerful and relevant!

In our experience, whether we are coaching or offering direct support, the solution to every problem we've encountered has been in the room with us. Similarly, the solutions to your problems—as a leader and as a person—lie within *you*.

Still, everyone needs a little help sometimes! So, we encourage you to reach out. Our certified SCQ facilitators offer sessions to guide organizations and individuals that seek to cultivate human potential, assist them in becoming more influential, and develop mechanisms to create sustainable legacies. You can set up a time to connect with our team at https://scquotient.com.

Thanks for reading. We hope you'll continue on your SCQ journey with us!

SOURCE LIST

Bandura, A. (1999). Social Cognitive Theory of Personality. *Handbook of Personality*, 2, 154–96.

Berger, W. (2014). *A More Beautiful Question: The Power of Inquiry to Spark Breakthrough Ideas*. Bloomsbury Publishing USA.

Carr, E., Reece, A., Kellerman, G. & Robichaux, A. (2019). The Value of Belonging at Work. *Harvard Business Review*. Retrieved from https://hbr.org/2019/12/the-value-of-belonging-at-work.

Daniel, G., & Goleman, D. (2006). *Social Intelligence: The New Science of Human Relationships*. Bantam Dell Pub Group.

Dickmann, M. H., & Stanford-Blair, N. (2002). *Connecting Leadership to the Brain*. Corwin Press.

Geisel, T. S. (1990). *Oh, the Places You'll Go!*. Random House Books for Young Readers.

Hess, F. M. (2013). *Cage-Busting Leadership*. Harvard Education Press.

Jensen, D. (2014). Churn: The High Cost of Principal Turnover. *School Leaders Network*. Retrieved from https://connectleadsucceed.org.

Lencioni, P. (2006). *The Five Dysfunctions of a Team*. John Wiley & Sons.

Lencioni, P. M. (2012). *The Advantage: Why Organizational Health Trumps Everything Else in Business*. John Wiley & Sons.

Maxwell, J. C. (1993). *Developing the Leader Within You*. Harper Collins.

Sahlberg, P. (2014). *Finnish Lessons 2.0: What Can the World Learn from Educational Change in Finland?*. Teachers College Press.

Thurman, H. (1996). *Jesus and the Disinherited*. Beacon Press.

INDEX

J–K

L

AUGUSTINE EMUWA

Augustine "Augie" Emuwa has dedicated his life to social impact work as both an educator and an entrepreneur. Raised by a single father who migrated from Nigeria to the south side of Chicago, Augie learned to adapt to conflicting cultural worlds at school, in his social circles, and in his neighborhood. Indeed, for Augie, adaptability became a means for acceptance, opportunity, and in some cases, survival. The juxtapositions of his childhood provided Augie with a special intuition that has guided his professional efforts to surface solutions in the realm of human and social capital. In Augie's eyes, equity and reconciliation aren't just thoughts; they represent a spirited outcry for investment and collective impact.

Currently, Augie is the founder and principal consultant of Identity Capital Consulting in Chicago, IL. Prior to that, Augie served in Chicago Public Schools—the third largest school district in the United States—as a teacher, behavior support specialist, literacy coach, assistant principal, and principal. In his administrative roles, Augie was instrumental in turning around failing schools at the elementary and high school level by helping to increase graduation rates and decrease suspension rates—without sanctioned governance from the state. These leadership experiences revealed a pathway for Augie into the field of social impact innovation.

Augie believes that schools and other organizations dedicated to serving kids can help shape equity in the U.S. and abroad, if scalable mechanisms are put in place. Through his experiences as a graduate, teacher, administrator, and parent, Augie has developed a keen awareness of what school should look and feel like from a whole-child perspective. His parallel experiences as a person and a practitioner fuel his desire to improve the lives of those serving and being served within schools and communities by supporting and coaching "hands on" leaders and teams. His personal philosophy is simple: The assets are in the room, as long as we listen, learn, and leverage.

Augie holds a bachelor's degree in marketing and management from Jackson State University, a master's degree in teaching with a focus on diverse learning, and an additional master's degree in school administration and organizational change, both from Roosevelt University. Additionally, Augie completed direct leadership training through a national principal selection residency founded at Harvard University.

Apart from these experiences, Augie's most significant accomplishments are being a husband to his wife, Sylvia, and a father to his four children, Brennan, Tatum, Lauren-Chima, and Benjamin the Tremendous Toddler. As a family, their commitment to work-life integration has been a parable of sorts for true happiness and passion, illustrated by the mantra, "Find a need, and fill it!"

Quirky Hobbies: Dreaming about tiny homes, hand-making bow ties, and writing!

JUSTINE GONZALEZ

Justine Gonzalez is a Chicago-based entrepreneur who supports K–12 school districts through her consulting firm, EducatorAide. She has published numerous articles, has been a guest on multiple podcasts, and writes a monthly column for the *Indianapolis Recorder*. Justine has served as a teacher, instructional coach, and K–12 school and district-level administrator in both Chicago and Indianapolis. As a third-culture kid born and raised in northern Indiana to her Puerto Rican father and Amish/Mennonite-background mother, she is intimately familiar with navigating cultural dissonance personally as well as through her educational experiences in public schools.

After teaching and coaching in Indianapolis Public Schools, Justine was accepted to the nationally acclaimed New Leaders Principal Residency program in Chicago. Afterward, she served as an administrator in the Chicago Public Schools' turnaround network. Some career highlights have included turnaround efforts in both classroom and administrator roles yielding results such as 90% of all K–1 students reading at or above grade level at a chronically failing elementary school in Chicago Public Schools, implementing previously non-existent bilingual programming, increasing enrollment, and growing community partnerships.

Following her time in Chicago, she became a founding principal for a network of schools focused on disengaged youth (dropout status or incarcerated) in Indianapolis and East Chicago. Within one year, she was promoted to serve as a regional director (superintendent) for 10 high-school campuses across Indiana, developed the New Teacher Cohort program and training model, and cultivated multiple campus partnerships.

Justine currently volunteers as a founding board member for Midwest Center for Social Services. She also partners with organizations to cultivate culturally connected, inclusive, and equitable learning and working environments through her consulting firm, EducatorAide. She is a PhD candidate, with a body of research that focuses on cultural neuroscience, cultural psychology, and cross-cultural communications.

With a creative spirit fueled by various entrepreneurial efforts, Justine is the best-selling co-author of the 2018 book, *Wealth for Women*. In addition, she co-hosts "The Sunflower Society" podcast with her sister, Kara. As a millennial leader devoted to equity, social impact, and liberatory transformation, Justine continues to prove that humans are multi-faceted and do not need to be boxed in or constrained to one single lane. Her message consistently helps others develop their self-awareness to maximize and leverage their spiritual gifts to affect the world in positive ways. Justine resides in the greater–Chicago area with her partner, Scott, and is a proud auntie to her nieces and nephews.

Quirky Hobbies: Brewing coffees with different media (i.e., pour-over, Greca, French press, etc.) and watching documentaries!